Prologue

Roasting chestnuts and crisp evergreen wafted through the crowded house, tickling the noses of the taller men who stood in the parlor smoking long pipes and comparing the year they had apart. Pots, pans, and laughter clattered from the kitchen as the women put the finishing touches on a large, perfectly cooked bird, dusted flour off onto their aprons as they rolled cookies, and scolded each other for dirtying their best dresses. Overdressed children wove through their legs as they chased a scared furry animal who only wanted to find a safe place to hide from the jolly chaos.

Tucked between the roaring fire framed in dark brick, and a green Sprula heavily covered in lace, handmade ornaments, and shimmery strings, sat a woman in a wicker rocking chair. Too old to socialize with the family, she slowly rocked in her corner under a half-finished quilt, the needle and thread almost slipping from her wrinkled fingers as she drifted in and out of sleep. Silver hair was bound tightly in a bun on the top of her head, pulling the wrinkles on her face almost painfully.

Shattering glass broke through the hustle and bustle, bringing the house to a stand still.

"Damn it Gregory, how many times have I told you not to touch the pictures!" A man yells out at a small yellow haired boy.

"Please father…" His small hands clutched a very worn out sketch of a beautiful, light haired woman with soft, perpetually happy grey eyes. The simple, dark wood frame still had the last shards of glass clinging to the corners. He ducked under the long dining room table to avoid his father's falling hand, but wasn't watching where he was going and bumped into the rocker when he came out. The old woman let out a small "oof" as she shook awake, the boy and his father both froze at the sound. The boy looked up at her with his small blue eyes full of tears that had yet to fall. "Please Grandmother, I didn't mean to break it, I just wanted to see her better, she is so beautiful and…" he stopped as his voice cracked and the tears began to slide down his cheek.

The old woman leaned forward, wiping his tears with her weathered thumb before taking the picture from his hands. Looking down at the beautiful woman filled her with feelings and memories of a time long gone, and a smile stretched across her face.

"It's quite alright Gregory. Would you like to know who she was?" He nodded as he tried to clear his sniffles and wipe his nose on his little jacket sleeve. She lifted him up onto her lap, making sure he was settled before raising her voice so all could hear. "Gather round children,

Winter's Heir

I have a story to tell you of how our family came to be."

Movement erupted as chairs and boxes and whatever else they could find were dragged across the solid wood floor, everyone scrambling for the best place to hear the woman speak. Even the older men acted like children, shoving each other aside for the seat with the best view. It had been a long time since Grandmother had a story to tell, and her tales of the older days never disappointed.

"This is a story of hate, greed, fear, anger, jealousy... but with all of the bad that your story has in it, this *is* Da'nu and in Da'nu there is love... and as we all know, love always wins."

Chapter One

Tucked into the eastern edge of Autumn Fall, where falling leaves kiss against the bitter winter chill of their mountainous neighbor, an orchard laid sleeping on rolling hills, blissfully indifferent to the disappearing starlight. Limbs hung low as bunches of over-ripened fruit bent them into sagging arches, bowing with the weight of their burden. The warm harvest sun streaked through the perfectly planted rows, casting long shadows over the painted landscape as it gently peeked over the horizon. Low drum beats in the far-off distance gave the land a heartbeat as it emerged from the darkness.

Leaves danced with gleaming shades of pumpkin orange and honeysuckle, each twirling through the air as they found themselves in freefall. While some landed in piles not far from the start, others found themselves drifting under the youngest branches of an unassuming Apula tree, one of many in the countless rows that stretched across the valley and settled on the shadow of a knight.

Cedric's black and dented helm sat beside him in the low, golden grass, revealing a dusty, battle-scarred face that hung down almost to his knees as he sat against the tree. His youth hid behind the marks that criss crossed his features.

A black-steel gauntlet covered his hand as it slowly pushed back his dirty-brown hair, streaks of sunny blonde catching the early light and shining like golden string.

He was worn and weary, the gift of sleep hadn't come for days as he tried to stay ahead of the king's army. Only when exhaustion caused him to trip over his own feet did he finally decide to stop, but only long enough to catch his breath.

But as the sun drifted over the gilded landscape, his armor felt like it weighed more than a horse, and he couldn't find the motivation to move again. He knew his quest was too much for the time he had to do it in. One week had already passed since he overheard the king's plans to marry his beloved.

He had been standing outside of a bathhouse high in the Autumn hills when he heard the right hand of the king proclaim the news. Although the conversation didn't involve him, it had been so loud, it echoed through the stone house and out to Cedric's ears.

"Word has arrived from King Korva! We are to return and serve as his wedding protection. Spring will unite with Summer!" Cheers erupted through the room, but the cold zing of dread rising from his gut urged him into action. The

Winter's Heir

Fair Lady of Spring Meadows, the very woman he had dedicated his life and purpose to, was betrothed to another. Betrothed to the only person he had any respect for, King Korva.

    Cedric had never felt a feeling like the one he got when he had first seen Petal Dancer. His troop had been assigned as the protection detail of the Spring Festival parade last year, and as usual young Cedric stood next to King Korva as the Rulers walked through the streets, the people throwing petals into the air over their heads. Through a curtain of pink and white, the most beautiful woman Cedric had ever seen emerged. Her golden hair shone like the sun, swaying with her every step down to the small of her back. Her lips were as red as the roses of the inner gardens. Her beauty had struck him so completely, Cedric had forgotten what he was doing entirely, catching the toe of one foot onto the heel of the other and smashed his face into the dirt. Her laugh rang like wedding bells in a church, and in that moment Petal became the last woman Cedric ever wanted, and he would do everything he could to become the best and strongest man he could, then he would ask her for her hand.

He had spent most of his life as a fighter, taking on the biggest and strongest opponents in order to prove himself to his king. All he had ever known was the bloodshed of the Arena where he had grown up, or the pride of conquering a town in the name of Korva. The most beautiful thing he had ever known was the way blood dripped from his blade in the early morning light after a successful raid, or the cheer of a crowd as he stood in front of the corpse of a captured beast. Yet, since that fateful day when his eye fell upon the stunning ruler of Spring Meadows, he could think of nothing else. Dream of nothing else except for the future they would have together once he had the prestige behind him to properly gain her hand.

Now he ran, daring to run faster than the whole armada and cavalry, as he deserted his post so that he may claim the Fair Lady before the king himself even had a chance to realize what he had done. He could not lose her, he wouldn't be able to survive.

Now that he had taken a moment to rest, the twist of hunger in his gut was overwhelming. He had been unable to stop after he fled the army he once commanded, only grabbing a bit of fruit off the trees as he ran. He dared not cry, nor show in any way the despair that crept into his heart. The dogs of the king's army smell tears and track fear, and they surely must know by now of his crimes.

He believed not in fate, although on this day, it may be the one thing that saved him.

Winter's Heir

"Woe is ye..." he whispered to the wind, "for it shall be an eternity before I have a chance to gaze upon that undying sunrise of beauty, my Fair Lady of Spring Meadows." There was a dull scraping as the plates of his battered and charred armor ground together between his back and the bark of the apula tree.

The Spirit of the Wind carried his words with an ever so playful echo down the endless rows of the orchard, twisting and twirling through the air.

Chapter Two

The smooth feminine hand of the Gypsy Witch was shrouded in an ivory glow as she reached up and grasped a violet peora fruit in the early morning light. Bracelets of stones and colorful cord wrapped around her wrist and down her arm. She wore clothes that were earth toned, layered together in torn sections to make a flowing dress so beautiful, it seemed even the trees were envious of the way it shifted and flittered. Her hair was as dark as a raven, and although a few ends hung over her face and down her neck, it sat with a messy elegance, twisted with a crown of vines and dandelions high on her head.

The wind swiftly danced through the trees, playing with the frayed ends of her dress before rising up to twirl the stray bits of her hair.

"Spirit of the Wind, what burden of the world do you place on me this day?" She sighed softly, lifting both arms and closing her hazel eyes to listen to the childish laughter that was the wind.

"Come, sweet Witch!" the wind whispered into her ear. "The Knight of Darkness sits just beyond this hill, tired and worn from his travels and in need of your guidance."

"The Knight of Darkness…in my own wood!" She exclaimed with a gentle smile, her lips glistening in a fiery shade of amber. Picking up her woven basket brimming with fruits of every color, she balanced it on her hip and took off at a deer's pace, following the wind as it led her through the orchard.

She slowed as she approached him, bare feet gently padding the earth. He sat with his hands over his face, curling into himself in a crumpled heap on the edge of tears. She could barely believe how much he had grown, had it really been that long? She thought of the baby swaddled in furs as she carried him to his new home, of the thin boy with the fighting spirit she would steal time to see as he grew. She had lost track of him as he became a man, but there before her, she could see the resemblance. He was scared, damaged even, but he was still her Cedric.

"Come now, Knight. Rise to your feet. What makes your soul so weary and your woe so great?"

He startled at the sound of her voice, thinking for a moment the hounds and army had caught up to him. The woman before him wasn't particularly stunning, but she was tall and moved with a grace he could barely comprehend. He had seen the image of this woman a thousand times in paintings and sculptures all through Autumn Fall, but he was still shocked that she stood there in the flesh. His heartbeat quickened, and he sat there frozen before her free hand took his and weightlessly guided him to standing. They saw eye to eye, he in all his metal plate and chain becoming just a hair's breadth taller than she.

"Oh Witch, what isn't there to woe over?" he began, relieved to have someone he could explain his story to. "My Fairest Lady, source of all my desires, is a two-month ride from this spot. I have no steed which makes the trek even greater, and the king's army is on my tail to imprison me as we speak for even daring to run to her. I fear I will never have the chance to proclaim my affections to my Lady of Spring Meadows.

"And if I do not find a way, she will be betrothed to another before the time comes that I may be free and able to gaze upon her face once more."

His weary eyes stared into hers, the last glint of hope slipping away as the despair of his situation finally set in. But the Witch, her eyes shining with the glimmer and sparkle of all the stars of the night, smiled lightly as an idea came to her. Perhaps she could solve two problems, and Cedric would be just the man to do it.

"I know of a mighty steed that can get you to Spring Meadows within two fortnights. He is fast and as strong as they come, but I must travel with you to bring him home." The knight was speechless at her offer, but a great burden was visibly lifted from his soul.

"Come now," the Witch urged. "He lives not far from here." She turned and walked off without a backward glance. The knight scrambled to grab his helmet and took off after her, leaving all his doubts and inhibitions at the base of the tree.

Chapter Three

The Gypsy Witch and the Knight of Darkness came upon a hill after some time. Purple, blue, and yellow wildflowers almost completely obscured the golden grass from view, as flutter bugs danced from one petal to the next. Here at the top of the hill, the Witch came to a stop with the Knight of Darkness only a few steps behind. Just beyond where they stood, the thick, twisted roots of the Mother Tree jutted from the ground, marking the division between territories.

The Witch lifted her arms, palms to the sky, and gently asked, "Come, Snow Bringer. Garuk, Cea'em Two'um!"

Winter's Heir

In response to the witch's words, a bitter chill ran through the colorful valley, bending the flowers and flattening the short grass in obedience to the cold. Thunder whispered in the distance, quickly gaining in speed and intensity until it was an overwhelming roar. A gigantic beast, mighty and almost pure white, leapt on six heavy hooves over the thick roots and pounded up the hill, pride flowing through his icy mane.

His breath poured out of his snout, so cold it frosted the air in a smoky haze. He left hoof shaped ice in his steps and a gentle flurry swirled in his wake. Saddled with thick gray furs of the mighty Tar'una wolf, a beast that roamed the wilds of the snow-covered Winterlands.

Snow Bringer pounded to a stop, his six hooves pawing at the now frozen grass in turn.

The Witch reached out her hand and cradled his snout, motioning for the knight to come to the beast with the other. He did, almost shaking but swallowed down his fear until it stuck firmly in his throat.

Snow Bringer, eyeing him intently with glowing red eyes marked with a glint of distress, examined the knight standing before him. He could smell the Winter in the man, but he had learned to trust no one. Cedric reached out his hand, causing Snow Bringer to rear backward, lifting his massive four front hooves to paw at the air above the knight's head.

The ground shook as he came down inches from Cedric's armor-plated boots. Cedric managed not to flinch in panic. Instead, he smiled as he reached out his hand once more to comfort the beast standing before him.

Winter's Heir

There was an almost eerie silence as unbridled power and battle-hardened skill leveled out to become equals. Snow Bringer, as fearful and massive as he was, gave in to the offer of friendship from the knight. As Snow Bringer's velvety snout connected with the cold black metal of Cedric's gauntlet, an immense burst of frozen energy shook out from his and Cedric's core. Freezing everything within thirty yards into a permanent winter oasis.

Turning towards the Witch with a puzzled look on his face, Cedric began to ask what had happened, but the Witch stopped him with a kind smile.

"I can see your questions like they were written on your skin, but now is not the time nor place to answer them. Our window of opportunity is small and closing fast. We must go now or risk time catching us before we are done. The Spring Festival waits for no man."

The beast bowed onto two knees, and the knight, although covered in his armor, swung onto its back with a heavy grace. He almost became part of Snow Bringer, and the red in the animal's eyes faded out to reveal a sapphire blue.

With perfect elegance the Witch glided onto the furry saddle, resting on the base of the first set of shoulders in front of Cedric, her hands intertwining in the snowy mane. Without a moment of hesitation, she demanded. "The Forest of All, Cea'em Two'um!"

Snow Bringer snorted loudly, and they were off, faster than the knight had dreamed to go, heading towards the dark tree line to the south. Before long, the constant rhythmic drumming of six hooves against dirt brought the tempting feeling of sweet sleep to Cedric, one that he could ignore no longer.

Chapter Four

Sudden, jarring silence woke Cedric roughly from his pleasant dream of dancing with his yellow-haired love. Had it been hours, or days since he had gotten on the back of the icy beast? All he knew was that the lulling movement had ended, and they were at the beginning of a thick, wall-like forest. The sun had just begun to settle over the horizon, with the outermost branches of the Mother Tree casting their ominous shadows before them.

"Do you know the place that lays before us, Cedric?" The Witch's hand slowly motioning to the trees.

"Only in name, I've never entered the forest before."

Dark fog rolled out from the tree line, thick and moving like it had a life of its own. The harder one tried to look into the forest, the less one saw.

"Stories of this place are old as the Mother Tree herself. One could get lost within the first few feet of entering the tree line and wander for years. Trees are said to be able to uproot and move when you're not looking, as if they have a life of their own. Thick fog can shape itself into your worst fear, or greatest desire, anything to daze and confuse all who dare to enter the heart of the forest to harm the Mother Tree.

Without a guide, you are doomed to be hopelessly lost in the darkness of your own mind. Not to mention the legions of creatures that live within the dark wood.

At least, that's what the stories say."

"The Forest of All." He whispered.

Winter's Heir

With a soft, padded thud, the Gypsy Witch dismounted from Snow Bringer and took a few steps forward, coming within inches of the tendrils of fog that acted like they were trying to reach out and grab her ankles. She clutched a small piece of antler tied around a crowded necklace and bowed her head.

Unsure of what he should be doing, Cedric shifted his weight uncomfortably. A crow rang out, then two, then three each farther from the last deeper into the wood. A few tense moments passed before a figure formed from the depths of the forest. Tall and broad, a crown of interlocking antlers defining his shadow. A bow could be seen slung over the shoulder, a quiver of arrows at the waist.

The Hunter emerged from the wood, furred leather-bound feet making no sound in the dry leaves and fallen branches. Piercing emerald-green eyes glancing only once at the knight and Cea'em Two'um, before settling on the Gypsy Witch.

Though he stood much taller and wider than her, he took a knee and bowed his head. His cape of moss and leaves trailed behind him, small dark fur faces adorning the shoulders and kissed at his chest. His curly, brown hair framed his lightly bearded face as he placed the antler crown lightly on the golden grass to his side, a show of respect normally reserved for royalty alone.

"M'Lady," he kept his tone soft for the Witch, his voice deep and gravelly, like a man who didn't have much opportunity to speak, "what a pleasant surprise to hear your call. I have missed your gentle presence." He took her small hand in his, kissing her knuckles before he rose to his feet, donning his crown once more. "What do you ask of me, sweet sorceress?"

The Gypsy's cheeks flushed before responding, "We are in need of passage through the forest, straight through to Spring Meadows." She glaned behind her to the knight still sitting on Snow Bringer before she turned back and whispered to the Hunter, "A few loose strings of fate to bond, I think."

The Hunter sighed deeply, knowing the Witch was up to her old tricks again. One simple nod, and he turned back to face the forest. He gave a long, low whistle through his fingers, and a distant grunt responded. A shadow formed between the branches; it was tall, taller than any horse, with antlers so large and spaced, it had to bend its head to and fro to avoid low hanging tree limbs. Another deep grunt as the Mighty Stag left the tree line and walked to the Hunter's side.

Winter's Heir

The animal's fur was coarse and deep brown, almost black in some spots as he shook out the morning dew that had settled on it. An aged leather saddle lay strapped to its back and almost blended into his coat, and a sturdy vine bridle wrapped around the velvety head, and reins sat at the base of the massive shoulders. As the beast knelt, the Hunter turned and mounted the Mighty Stag, who pranced and snorted, trying to get back into the cover of the trees. The Witch in turn mounted Snow Bringer, and the knight leaned forward to whisper in her ear, "What happens now?"

"Now, we follow."

Chapter Five

Hooves crunched against old leaves as the small troop passed through the fog into the first ring of the Forest of All. The darkness of night fell over them like a blanket, caressing the sleeping trees and thickening the air almost as well as the fog that now swirled around the ground in small pools. The Hunter and his Stag led the way, his cape flowing over the back of the mighty animal and settling in layers on its rump. Snow Bringer followed close behind, large hoof prints of ice the only evidence of their passing.

"Much has changed since your last coming, as I am sure you have noticed, Enchantress." The Hunter spoke softly but his low voice carried behind him.

"Brave Hunter, you have been hard at work, I presume?" the Gypsy Witch responded in her sweet tone.

"Alas, though I wish to take the credit for this wonder, it was not I." He turned in his saddle to look at Cedric and the Witch. "A great shift is to blame, one I have not seen in many years. The fates may finally be on our side again."

The Witch nodded, and the Hunter turned back. Cedric, more confused than ever, spoke his thoughts.

"Great shift? Fates? I fear I do not understand."

"You will in time, Sir Knight. Patience is not your strong suit." The Witch looked over her shoulder at him. "This first ring that we are in now was for a long time one of the most terrifying places in all of Da'nu. But as you can see..." she lifted an arm to point to the petrified landscape around them, "most of the evil has returned to the inner rings. Life will grow anew here, and it will become the thriving sanctuary it was so long ago."

As the Knight looked closer, he could see small sprouts of leaves budding from the long-dormant trees and meager beginnings of blossoms at the ends of their branches. He had never known the Forest of All to be anything but a terrible, destructive place. 'A stain on the center of the map,' his king had called it once before. The thought that it had been more than a dark, dead forest like he had been told it was since he was a boy baffled him into stunned silence as he looked around.

"Woah..." The Hunter and his Stag came to a silent stop, Snow Bringer a step later as the

Gypsy pulled back on his mane. There was an edge of caution to the Hunters tone.

Time stood still as the Hunter pulled his bow from his shoulders softly and slowly to not make a sound. All Cedric could hear was his heart drumming in his ears against his metal helm as anticipation rose in the dead air. He reached for his sword that was normally at his side and quickly remembered he didn't have one. A feral squeal almost made him jump, his armor creaking, and he could see what the Hunter had stopped them for.

A huge, tusked animal turned and looked directly at the Knight. Anger flashed in the boar's eyes as it pawed the ground ready to charge. The Knight froze in terror, but the Hunter spurred to action, pulling a black wood arrow with a razor sharp tip from the quiver at his side, docking and drawing his bow in one smooth motion.

Without even one breath the arrow was in flight, burying deep into the chest of the boar. A shrill squeal sent shivers down Cedric's spine as he watched the heavy animal pull back before falling to the side, skin twitching and legs jerking as they held onto life.

The Hunter dismounted and bounded to the animal, expertly unsheathing a silver dagger and sliced through the tough skin of the neck. Blood sputtered out in the dim moonlight and the boar's body finally gave in to its fate. A faint wisp of white smoke left the nostrils and flew up into the canopy of the forest, its soul leaving the body and returning to the Mother Tree.

They sat in silence again as the Hunter finished his task and cleaned his blade and arrow on his pant leg. He lifted the boar and draped it over the rump of the Stag, the mighty animal not even flinching at the added weight.

"That will make a fine meal, Brave Hunter," said the Witch, her pride in him seeping into her words.

"It will be something, though not enough I'm afraid." His voice was reverent and calm, heavy with the life he had taken. The Stag twisted his antlers around for the Hunter to use as a handle, and he remounted without another word. They continued forward, the six-legged horse and its occupants a few steps behind. Before long, an orange light could be seen flickering through the trunks.

"Your camp is full again?" the Gypsy Witch exclaimed, a touch of disbelief in her voice.

Winter's Heir

"Much has changed since your last coming, Enchantress."

Chapter Six

The rich smell of roasting pork and root vegetables floated through the camp as Cedric pulled his armor off piece by piece next to a roaring fire. Some of the buckles were stuck to the leather and he realized he hadn't had a chance to remove and oil it in over a week. His body felt light and free without the added weight, but his cloth underclothes were stained with sweat and musky, even stiff in places. As he looked around the thriving camp, he wondered if he could find someplace to wash his dirty garb.

People of all races and colors were busy with chores and activities every way he looked. Some bronze-skinned women wove baskets from the long grass, laughing and gossiping in a tongue that sounded rough and broken to his ears. Men without shirts made pikes and dug trenches around the camp to place them in, making Cedric wonder what lived in the woods that required those kinds of defences. Still others carried wood to piles near the many burning fires, and the sound of metal hitting metal rang clear as someone, somewhere worked a forge. There wasn't a lot of people, but enough that the camp was busy with movement, even in the cover of night.

The Witch was helping a young, light-haired girl turn a pig spit over one of the smaller cooking fires when the Hunter grabbed her arm and pulled her into a tent across the path.

Hand woven blankets and rugs covered every surface in the small, dark space. One dimly lit lantern sat on a small wooden table, casting everything in a faint golden glow. A well used loom sat against the far wall, a project half started in blues and reds waiting for it's maker to return.

"Why have you not told him yet? There is nothing to be running from. The king cares not of his whereabouts, but he will for certain be killed if he reaches his end, and that is only if Petal has any feelings for that boy at all." His emerald eyes burned into hers.

"Hunter, I..." She looked away.

"You are twisting fates again, aren't you? Bending the power of Da'nu and the Mother Tree for your own bidding, as if you do not remember what happens when you push it too far."

"I am NOT abusing the Mother Tree's power!" Now it was her turn to glare at the Hunter. "Cea'em Two'um needed a Guardian, I simply joined them. I am helping the fates, not twisting them into my own image as the one you so cruelly attempt to compare me to!"

"And who exactly is this knight you have bonded to Snow Bringer? It can't be just anyone."

"That, Brave Hunter, is the Knight of Darkness, firstborn son of the late Winter King and the Summer Queen." His forehead wrinkled as surprise swept over the Hunter's face.

"That thin boy is the Heir of Winter? I believed him to be dead the night his father was murdered and his mother died."

"Everyone believes he is dead. I stole him away that dreadful night and hid him among the farmers. I lost track of him for a time but none of that matters now. He is here, he is alive, and the strings of fate can weave together again as they always should have."

The Hunter shook his head in disbelief.

"Every time I see you, Enchantress, you shock me. But you must tell him of his past. He knows nothing of his place in this world, and you can't keep leading him on like a stray dog after a bone." She absentmindedly picked some dirt out from under one of her fingernails as she mulled over the idea.

"I suppose I can tell him... I was going to wait and have the Mother do it, but he probably won't be able to contain his questions that long." With the Gypsy Witch's words hanging in the air, the Hunter pulled her into his embrace, inhaling deeply as she melted into his strong arms. Her sweet maple and fruit scent overwhelmed him every time he could hold her this close.

He loved this trickster of a woman, almost as much as she loved taking lost strands of fate and twisting them back together. She was the wandering wind and would never settle, while he was the forest trees, strong and rooted in place. No matter how much he would wish it, their strands would never intertwine, but he savored every second they brushed together.

"You, Guardian of Autumn Fall, are a stunning woman," he whispered into her ear.

Chapter Seven

Crackles and pops exploded in small sporadic bundles from the main fire as it was quickly surrounded with people. The meat had finished cooking, and the morsels were shared around evenly on large, stiff leaves. It was barely more than a mouthful, but each seemed grateful as they talked and laughed and tried to find a good seat. The Witch and the Hunter joined the circle, he took a seat while she remained standing, walking close to the roaring fire.

"Tonight, I will tell the story of our world, from the beginning to current time." A hush fell over the people, the Knight especially as he watched the Witch grab a handful of dust from the satchel at her side. She threw it into the fire, causing thick smoke to plume over the roaring flames and settle over their heads in a cloud, changing color and shape as she spoke. The story was an old one, told to every child at least once at bedtime by their parent, but the Witch's voice made it sound like it had never been heard before.

"Many centuries ago, when Da'nu was calm and balanced, the Mother Tree stood tall and proud in the center of our world. Her branches were wide and full of life, her roots intertwining far throughout the lands, creating the border between regions where they jutted from the ground. She gifted each realm a Companion, a powerful and strong animal born from the power of the Tree herself. Given the task to choose for itself a Guardian, each Companion bonded with a being born from the human races that inhabited the lands.

Winter's Heir

"She created the violet fields and carved the river that floods Spring Meadows with the subtle growth of clover patches, which brought the birds and filled the air with their song." Rain Dancer, a winged horse was formed as the Companion of Spring, its flowing tail and feathers adorned with every color imaginable as it flew through the cloud of smoke. It's pearly iridescent horn curled tightly around itself, cutting through the gray in a long, glistening line. "With a flap of her wings, a thunderous ovation can sweep through the land, causing showers to fall in her wake. Cea'dah Tep'um named Colla Tep'um, Petal Dancer, a kind and gentle soul chosen because of the love her people had for her.

"She formed the plains of the Summer Sanctuary, vibrant with mature, lush prairie grass and scattered it with Beyos and other grazing cattle." The Companion of Summer was a dragon, bright red and orange as the fire that burned in its gut, a streak of pure gold running from the tip of his nose down his sides and speckling out in the tail. "Sun Riser had wings so massive it could cast a shadow over a whole village, and breath hot enough to turn the very ground into liquid. Dar E'um named Leo'ra, Ember, for she was the wealthiest in all of Da'nu.

"Our Mother crafted the gentle rolling orchards of Autumn Fall, painted the trees in golden hues, and lured the playful wind." A massive owl wise and looming known as Wind Runner was the Companion of Fall, with shades of auburn and gold painting his feathers, and eyes a dazzling hazel. "Talons sharp enough to cut stone, yet gentle enough to rock a newborn babe. Coo'Rah Be'um named Coo'Har Be'um,

Gust Runner, a witch by birth gifted with grace and an ability to influence those around her.

"She rose the Winterland mountains and locked them in ice, filling it with furred and skilled hunting beasts of all sizes." The smoke twisted through forms of Snow Bringer, the Companion of Winter. His sapphire eyes and stark white mane glowing as he cantered over their heads. "Cea'em Two'um named Cea'ra Diem, Frost Slayer, a warrior known throughout the Winterlands for his strength and courage."

The Witch's voice grew louder.

"She filled The Forest of All with an abundance of wonderful, spiritual beings, and gave every inch of the forest her love and power."

Winter's Heir

Twin Mighty Stags were formed as the Companions of the Forest of All, each standing at least nineteen hands tall. "One white as the blossoms that once bloomed on the Mother Tree named Life Breather. The other, Life Taker, as dark as the shadows cast by her branches, chose twin brothers, one just seconds older than the other. The dark Fra Key'um named Dovah for his patience gained from years of stalking animals through the brush, and the white Fra Soo'um named the younger brother, Korva for the attention to detail and planning he put into everything he sought to accomplish." The smoke twisted and twirled through visions of glimmering forest-filled landscapes, swirling sprites, and dancing deer, all in harmony with each other.

"The Guardians took on the abilities of their Companions in time, each given a power helpful to the region they were sworn to protect along with elongated life.

"All lived in perfect harmony for many, many centuries." She paused for a moment to let the words sink in, especially to the Knight, who would be hearing this other half of their worlds history for the first time.

"But this was not destined to last for all eternity."

The smoke billowed black and dark, consuming the first images as they tried to scatter away without success. "The second born of the twins could not be content in his place in the world. The beings he was tasked with creating were ugly in his eyes, too soft and kind for his liking. He chose his own path, away from the way the Tree had given him and took the creatures and twisted them into what he saw fit." Again, the smoke shifted, images of terrifying animals, just skin and bones and at times, no skin at all with glowing, red eyes filled the air.

"This satisfied him for a time, and he was able to hide his creations from the Mother. But he grew restless quickly, his manipulations were not enough for the growing evil within him. One day without any forethought, he turned his twisted spirit on his Companion." The smoke ran deep red and filled the air over their heads like a cloud of blood.

"He attempted to change Life Breather, and it died at his hand with a piercing screech that rang through all the souls of Da'nu. Without the Companion, his power was stripped from him in that moment, and a great shift shook the land. The Mother Tree could ignore the darkness within him no longer. She called to the other Guardians in their tongue. 'Garuk!'"

All around the fire jumped as she yelled the ancient word. By now, they all spoke in hushed whispers if they spoke at all, comforting those beside them with held hands, and all attention was on the Witch and her smoke.

"We came as fast as we could…" Her voice sobered as the smoke swirled, and the Knight could see a line of Guardians and Companions rushing to the Tree, the owl and dragon flying above the two horse-like beings, the Mighty Stag leading the charge.

"We came to Her just as he did, the dark evil inside him seeped from his mouth in a thick black fog, the legion of twisted half-dead creatures at his heels to defend him. We fought as hard as we could, but we were losing, as the ground at our feet shook." The smoke swirled through images of giant rock statues emerging from the ground in the heat of the battle.

Winter's Heir

"The Mother Tree had called the Drum'ma from the earth, giant stone beings to stand at our side and together, we forced the fallen Guardian from the forest." All gasped and cheered as the smoke showed the brother crossing out of the fores t into the endless frozen drifts of the Winterlands.

"Although we evicted this great evil from our forest…" She gave a moment for the cheering to calm down. "…the scars of his presence have not left. The beings Korva twisted still roam our wilds, and the dark smoke still swirls upon our dirt, reminding us at every step the uphill battle we have to face to restore normality." The camp was quiet, every head bowed at her words. "Many of you have been raised in this madness, born into this world, and it is all you have ever known… The Winter and Summer Kingdoms fell to his evil hand. Autumn Fall feels the effect of his reach, and soon Spring Meadows will be engulfed into his rule. Nothing will stop him from coming for the Mother Tree.

"But fear not, for a great shift is occurring! For in your mist sits the Son of the Winter King, thought lost in the tragedy that befell his father and mother, but alas no more!" The Gypsy stared straight at the knight, and all at once, he knew she was talking about him. "Cea'em Two'um, Snow Bringer, has accepted the knight as his Guardian. We have begun a quest for him to win his destined Fair Lady, the Queen of Spring Meadows. If there are any who wish to join us through the inner rings to the Mother Tree, let these words stand as your invitation." With that, she turned and left the circle.

Chapter Eight

Cedric was left confused and a bit dazed after the Witch's story by the fire. The next hour or so was a blur as people came up to him wanting to speak, shake his hand, and some even just to touch his armor.

He tried to seek out the Witch but couldn't find her anywhere in the camp, and the Hunter, it seemed, had disappeared too. The sun began to peak through the trees in small streams that speckled the dirt around him. Noticing all manner of people yawning and going into their tents, Cedric realized that he was tired and should see if there was a spare tent he could lie in until he could find the Witch. Picking up his armor in a bundle, he wandered the camp.

"Pardon me," he asked a woman ducking into her sleeping space. She paused and turned to look at him.

She was a slight woman, with black hair like the Witch's, but her stark-white skin brought out her violet eyes. "What can I 'elp you with?" she inquired.

"Miss, I was hoping there would be a spare tent where I may be able to lie my head for the... erm... day?"

The woman chuckled at Cedric's awkwardness but motioned for him to follow as she walked away down a path.

"Takes a little getting used to, but it's better this way," the woman said over her shoulder, "The beasties come out in the day."

"Beasties?"

"Weren't you listenin' to the Gypsy Witch? Twisted, awful creatures... I'd feel bad for um, but being they would kill us the second they had a chance, they can all feel the bite of a good blade. Took my brother, you know. And my closest friend."

A quiet, garbled cackle echoed through the forest then, far off but horrifying nonetheless. The woman stopped in her tracks so suddenly that Cedric had to swerve off the path to avoid bumping into her.

"See? Beasties." Picking up their pace once more, the woman rambled on, "I've never seen one up close. Don't plan on it neither. The 'unter keeps um at bay, bless him."

Cedric mulled over this as they walked seemingly out of the camp for a short time before coming to a wall of vine-like branches.

"This is where Guardians rest their 'eads. We all call it Guardian Grove. You'll find your place here."

She pulled aside the curtain and motioned Cedric inside.

"Thank you... Sorry, I am afraid I failed to ask your name."

"Naria."

"Thank you again, Naria. You can call me Cedric." She gave him an awkward, half smile before turning on her heel. Cedric watched, bemused, as Naria made the journey back to the main camp. He could honestly say he had never met someone quite like her, and he hoped they would have another chance to talk once he could ask the Witch some questions.

Cedric stood there watching her black hair flow behind her until she became hidden in the shadows of the dark wood. He let the curtain drop and looked around at the Guardian Grove.

Six hollow trees had grown together in a crescent shape to make six modest houses, all leaning in and supporting one another. Snow Bringer and the Mighty Stag grazed on the soft, dark grass at the center as light bugs buzzed and twinkled around their forms. The huge owl Wind Runner perched in the intertwining branches. He looked sleepily at Cedric before closing his hazel eyes and settling back down into slumber. Sunlight was just beginning to break, and ribbons of weak light made their way down from the canopy but dispersed before they ever reached the ground.

After staring for far too long at the surreal scene in front of him, Cedric could see the light of a fire burning through the open door of the middle house. He decided to look there for the Witch.

She was just finishing a root stew when the Dark Knight walked in. The Witch pointed just past Cedric without taking her eye off the boiling pot.

"Before we begin, grab that container over there on the top shelf. I saw you wanting to oil your armor. That should do the trick. It's purified pig fat with a dash of Velerio fruit for preservation."

He turned and saw a wall of shelves with a variety of vessels, jars, and containers filled with all kinds of dried herbs or liquid concoctions. Each one was individually tagged and labeled with care, some in the ancient language, others simply with hand-drawn pictures. In the middle of the topmost shelf was a clay jar, and he assumed that was the one she had meant. He placed his armor on the floor with a muted thud and carefully lifted the jar from its place, setting it onto the low table beside the fireplace.

"There should be some rags in that basket there," the Witch pointed, again without looking up, to just underneath the table. "Use as many as you need," she expressed, before walking away to grab some bowls from a low shelf across the room.

"I'm a bit confused, Witch…" Cedric said after sitting down on a thick, fur rug and pulling his chest plate onto his lap.

"I know you are, Cedric. It's a confusing time we are living in. Especially you. You believed you were a farmer's son, did you not?" There was a small pause as she ladled stew into the wooden bowls.

"How do you know so much about me?"

"Sir Knight, I was there at your birth! It is not every other day when a child is born of two Guardians… A special day indeed."

"But how do you know that child is me? I know my father, he was a harsh man and by no means a king."

"You know the family I placed you with. Kempam and Durah, and their small daughter Tea'ala. Sweet people, loyal to the true Winter King even after he was slain." She handed him the full bowl and a hand-carved spoon, and he put aside the chest plate. "It was part of our agreement that it was not their place to mention any of this to you."

There was a dull scraping as Cedric pulled the last remnants of the stew into his mouth and before he could even ask the Witch, she had her hand out and stew in the ladle. She refilled his bowl and tore a large chunk from a slab of herb-covered flatbread roasting on a stone beside the roaring fire. He felt deeply disappointed in himself that he hadn't figured all this out on his own and had trouble meeting her eyes. If he was the son of two Guardians like the Witch claimed, wouldn't he have been able to feel it? Wouldn't he have been able to feel he was more than a farmer's son? Betrayal joined the mix of emotions in his head. How could they not tell him? How could his parents go years of beating his spirit into submission and seeing him sold off into the army without ever once telling him he had blood meant for greater things?

"So... they knew all along?" He tried his best to not make the words sound bitter.

"Oh, yes. But you have to understand, when a guardian such as myself arrives at your door with a babe in their arms, you do as they ask without many questions." She handed him the food and watched him devour the second helping of stew almost as fast as the first, using the bread to clean his bowl before consuming that too.

He hadn't eaten a good meal in over a week now, and the roasted pork in the camp had only teased his appetite. The stew was savory and warm, full of tender chunks of meat-like roots and juicy vegetables, and the growl of his stomach won over the thoughts swimming in his mind. After the third bowl with bread, he could finally slow down to polish and oil his armor again while taking bites of stew-soaked bread.

"You knew my birth parents then?" Cedric didn't want to leave the air hanging with his own self-reproach, so he tried to move the questions along. "What were they like?"

The Witch nodded. "Your mother was the Queen of Summer, gentle as the prairie grass but ruthless as the sun. She ruled with an iron fist and was bonded to Sun Riser, so she had a taste for anything that glittered." She paused again to refill their bowls and set a black kettle to hang over the fire.

"Your father was a warrior, born and bred, and rose to his position through bloodshed. He had enough courage for a hundred men, and all in the Winterlands respected his rule. Snow Bringer would carry him here from time to time, as Sun Riser would carry his queen. I watched as the spark of love grew between them until it couldn't be ignored.

I will never forget the night they took the journey to the Mother Tree...." She trailed off for a moment as the kettle whistled loudly, and she grabbed two mugs from hooks above the fireplace. "It was a tradition in those days for Guardians, if you were to make a monumental decision that could change the course of the fates, you would travel to the Mother Tree for her advice." She placed the mugs on the table and walked behind Cedric to the shelves, grabbing a glass jar full of herbs with a simple label with a picture of a leaf drawn on it.

"They returned a week or so later. She still wore the crown of blossoms, with the added touch of delight written on their faces. The Mother allowed their marriage, and it was a most joyous day!" She wrapped a measured spoonful of herbs into a cloth, placing it into one of the mugs, then again for the other, before taking the hot kettle from the fire and pouring steaming water over the bundles. "Soon after that, everything changed."

"The betrayal of the Guardian, as was in your story by the fire?"

"Yes, that was the beginning of it. The great battle took place a few months after the wedding, and though the queen was a valiant fighter, she sustained several wounds that never healed. Your birth was just too much for her body to take—"

A loud grunt outside interrupted her thoughts, and the Hunter barged into the room, panic written on his face.

"Naria! Have you seen Naria? She is missing from camp."

"She led me here this morning," Cedric replied. "The last I saw she was on her way back to camp, but that was less than an hour ago."

"You let her go by herself?"

"Y...yes?"

The Witch's bowl dully clattered to the dirt floor as she turned and ran to the far corner, grabbing a twisted branch staff and a thick, metal longsword, tossing the latter to the Knight before running out the doorway. Cedric and the Hunter followed close behind.

It was about halfway down the trail when they stopped, the Hunter and the Witch taking a knee, noticing something was off in the dirt. She traced a paw print, almost as big as her hand, and pointed into the forest without a word. The Hunter rose and took a few steps forward before noticing the blood splatter around him and pointing to the smeared drag of red through the dead leaves.

Finally catching up to them, and seeing the tracks and the blood, realization swept over Cedric. With how much blood was painting the grass even if they did find Naria, she wouldn't survive long. He lurched forward, ready to follow the trail and kill whatever had invaded the camp, but the hard end of the Witch's staff against his chest stopped him in his tracks.

"Killing them will only bring more." Her voice was heavy and downcast.

The thick hand of the Hunter grabbed the front of Cedric's shirt as he rushed at him in less than a breath, pulling him close to his emerald eyes.

"You never, never let someone walk alone in the day. You cannot even begin to comprehend what your ignorance has cost us." Anger was evident in his deep voice. "You are not in the army now, boy. This is what your precious king has cursed us with. Countless creatures that will kill without a second thought when given the opportunity. I refuse to guide this bumbling idiot through the forest until he's had some kind of training. He'll get us all killed."

"He didn't know, Hunter. You can't place the whole blame on him."

"I don't." He sighed, letting go of Cedric's shirt. "I blame myself for giving the people here a false sense of security. I have done my job of protecting them too well, and I will deal with the camp, so this never happens again. I blame that damn woman. How careless she was being with her own life. I blame myself for thinking he would be smart enough to know of the dangers here. He knows nothing of what should be feared or fought… Mark my words, Witch, he will know before we go a single step deeper into the forest."

Chapter Nine

It had been several days since Naria had been killed, the first bloodshed in the Hunter's Camp in more than two years. Cedric slowly peeled his shirt from his skin with a groan of pain. The Witch was careful not to touch the black and blue splotches that covered his back as she examined him, knowing herself just how painful the Hunter's training could be. Blood trickled from the many deep cuts he had obtained, and his arms and chest were just as bad. He looked like he had been awake for weeks although he had slept the night before, the dark circles under his eyes dragging down almost to his cheeks.

Due to the sparse knowledge Cedric had about the beasts that lived in the Forest of All, the Hunter had been putting him through an intense and fast learning process, for his body and his mind.

"The only fighting I was trained for was to fight people that were afraid… these beasts show no fear." He murmured over his shoulder.

"That is what sets them apart from the normal things you have had to kill." The Witch said while grabbing a clay pot from a shelf and began rubbing the thick green contents into the cuts and bruises on Cedric's back. "The beasts you have been fighting the last few days are nothing compared to the ones that lie within the inner rings. Did he say you were doing well?"

Cedric shrugged. "He never says much of anything, besides scolding me when I have done something horribly. I suppose I am doing better as he is yelling at me less." He winced as the Witch rubbed the salve into a particularly deep cut on his shoulder.

"You must be more careful, Cedric. If the cuts are too deep, they will not heal for a very long time, if ever."

There was silence for a time as she worked her way down his battered back and arms, careful to get every laceration and bruise completely covered.

"Can you tell me of their death?" It fell out of his mouth before he had a chance to swallow it. He could never seem to keep quiet when he knew he should.

The Witch sighed deeply. "Your parents?" she questioned, although she already knew the answer. Cedric nodded before the Witch continued on, "It was a dark day. Both joyous and dark the day they died."

"How so?"

She grabbed some clean cloths from a bowl of water at their side, ringing them out before she answered, "It was only days after the battle at the Mother Tree... The King of Winter had only just made it back to his fortress when we got word that the Queen of Summer was in labor. We had pushed the fallen Guardian out into the Winterlands, a cold and unforgiving place in hopes he would wander until he perished from the cold. There had been no sightings of him, but no body had been found either, so he felt it best to return to the stronghold and wait for any word on Korva.

"I had rushed to the queen's side, and by the time I arrived, she was already near death. The midwives were unprepared for the sudden and hard labor that had come upon her, and the wounds had reopened... There was so much blood..." She gazed off for a moment as the memory rushed over her.

"There was nothing I could do to save her. She lived just long enough to birth her children, and I held her hand as the light left her eyes." Cedric looked at her puzzled.

"Wait… I'm sure I didn't hear you right. Did you say *children*?"

"Yes," the Witch smiled. "She gave birth to twins. A girl I named Reala, and you, Cedric."

"T-twins? I have a blood sister? Where is she? Is she here at the camp? Can I meet her?" His words poured out of his mouth so quickly, they all mashed together in a jumbled heap. He had a sister in Tea'ala, but she was considerably older than he and had never given him much more than the occasional smack on the back of the head. To know there was someone out there that shared his blood, to the point she had shared a womb with him, would have knocked him off his feet if he had been standing.

"With the queen's death, her riches and crown would fall to the next in line old enough to rule, and with the only heirs far too young, the rebel group from the south would come in any day. They would seek out any who could contest their rule, even for the future. For your safety, I stole you both away. Just as I hid you with Tempam and Durah, I hid your sister with a trusted family in the Summer Sanctuary, hoping that maybe one day, she could claim back the Summer throne. I lost track of her, as I did with you for a time. I was going to take you back to the castle in the Winterlands to be raised by the king's advisers, but as I crossed over the boundary, the wind told me the news." She stopped again to pick up her clay pot and put it back in its place.

"We had underestimated the fallen Guardian, and he had traveled straight to the Winter Mountains where the king's castle laid.

Slit Frost Slayer's throat while he slept." The Witch's eyes took on a faraway look as she shook her head. "I still have trouble accepting it, and it's been twenty-five years. The most powerful, courageous man ever born in Da'nu, slaughtered in his sleep like a hog, all whilst his wife died in childbirth." Cedric didn't quite know how to process this. From the moment he had found out that his true father had died, he had hoped that he had maybe done so in battle, been run through with a sword, or taken down by a beast, certainly not like this. Not killed in cold blood at his weakest point. He clenched his fist so tightly, the knuckles turned white, and his teeth ground together. He questioned why he had ever put his faith in such a vicious, hateful king, and couldn't help but wonder if that made him a bad person too.

Chapter Ten

"This is the last day we have to train. If you are to get to Spring Meadows before the wedding, we will have to leave soon." Cedric and the Hunter's blades sliced through the air, a sharp clink as they contacted one another again and again.

It had been two weeks since that first night by the fire and the death of Naria from his ignorance the next morning, and they only had that long to get through the Forest of All from one end to the other. Cedric could almost outmaneuver the Hunter now, his feet growing ever lighter and quicker in their matches. He could move silently through thick underbrush, right past a Howler and have it never even smell him. His chocolate-brown eyes had lightened around the outer edge into an icy blue, and the short beginning of a beard on his cheeks was speckled with white.

The two warriors circled and sparred with each other for several hours as the sun dipped below the horizon, as they had almost every day. With a twist and a clatter, Cedric's blade stopped at the Hunter's neck for the first time, nicking the skin and a small bead of red formed. The two men stood panting for a long moment, a small, rare smile breaking the Hunter's normally stone-cold face.

"I look at you, but I see your father's face looking at me."

"Did you know my father well, Hunter?" Cedric's blade fell to his side, and they stepped back from each other in the dirt ring.

"He did not like to get close to anyone, too much bloodshed too early in life; only the Summer Queen knew him well. But he was a great man. He would fight the Tar'una with his bare hands and laugh about it later over the fire. Anyone born and raised in the unending cold would be hardened and fearless, but your father was more than that, practically part beast."

They were both drenched in sweat, panting hard but content. "Come now, we will go to the Gypsy Witch and eat. I hear the camp is preparing a great feast to send us off."

As the two entered the main camp from the training ground, they were confronted by the smell first. Roasted fruits and meats lined a great wood table, and everyone went around, taking a little of everything as they conversed and laughed. Too consumed in their own conversations, most didn't even seem to notice as Cedric and the Hunter moved around the table. He hadn't had much time to get to know the many people that lived in the camp, but Cedric recognized a few as they came up to wish him well.

As everyone settled by the fire, Cedric picked a spot by a small tree, leaning up against it and relaxing a bit in the heat of the flames. His belly was full, and his muscles were tired; the warmth given off by the flickering flame weighed heavily on him. It was about the time when he would normally fall asleep in the Witch's house and after a long day of sparing and hunting, he didn't even fight the gentle call of dreams, the tree supporting his weight as he slipped away.

The party dragged on without him, and as warm mead was passed around even the Hunter laughed and danced as the Gypsy Witch thumped a slow beat on a drum. The night lumbered on, the air grew cold, but the warmth from the alcohol allowed the masses to ignore it. Frost crept through the camp unnoticed, covering each stick and mossy stone one by one in its icy embrace. Only when gentle flurries fell, and their breath fogged around them did anyone speak up. It started as just a confused murmur, whispered questions, confused faces and pointed fingers slowly elevating into wild panic as it snowed in the forest for the first time. People ran to their tents, unsure of the white specks falling from the skies but feeling like some kind of shelter would be safer from it.

The Witch jumped up and ran to Cedric's side, shaking him roughly until he awoke. The Hunter stood over him as his eyes shot open, now completely sapphire blue, and the flurries stopped as suddenly as they had begun. Cedric gasped for air like a fish pulled from the water. His arms flailed for a moment before gripping a fistful of the Hunter's shirt, desperate for anything to ground him in the present.

"You were dreaming, weren't you?" The Witch's voice was kind as she looked at Cedric and smiled.

This transformation time was nothing new to her. Every Guardian had gone through it, but it had been several centuries since she had witnessed it, warming her heart to see it before her.

"The fire was so warm, but I was too tired to move and…" He noticed the white that had accumulated on the branches and stones around him starting to drip as they melted, and slowly let go of the Hunter. "Was it snowing?"

"He is ready." The Hunter spoke as if to answer his question, abruptly turning and walking away. The Witch helped Cedric to his feet, and they walked out of the now empty camp, and down the path to the Guardian Grove.

Chapter Eleven

In the safety of the Witch's house, the black kettle whistled its piercing tune as she prepared three cups of tea.

"It is perfectly normal as you gain the attributes of your Companion to have little control of what you do. Give it time and grow close to Snow Bringer, he will help you make sense of it all." She looked up over Cedric's shoulder as the Hunter walked through the door, holding a long bundle wrapped loosely in white fur. Cedric rose and faced him as the Hunter held the parcel out for the knight to take.

"This, Cedric, was your father's. It was entrusted to me after his death, and you are now ready to wear it at your side." The fur covering fell open to reveal a white metal sheath, twisting ancient words etched down the middle and sapphire jewels decorating the sides. A thick hilt sat beside it, equally adorned but missing a blade as if it was broken off cleanly.

Cedric reached out his hand and grabbed the hilt, holding it up to examine it. Frost grew from his fingertips, strips of white chasing each other through the grooves and onto the base, building over itself as if the very air above it was freezing. He watched as a thick blade formed, as clear as ice but as thick as the hardened steel broadswords he had fought with in the army.

"Tonight is a special night indeed," the Witch spoke, breaking the trance Cedric had found himself in. He grabbed the sheath, slipping the mighty sword inside before taking the mug of tea the Witch offered him.

"Tonight and tomorrow you shall spend with Cea'em Two'um. You will find he will understand you better than you know yourself.

Winter's Heir

Tomorrow night, we leave for Spring Meadows." The Hunter put his rough hand on Cedric's shoulder, letting the fur covering fall to the ground. "I shall no longer call you Knight of Darkness, that role is long behind you. You are the Guardian of the Winterlands now, as you will be until your death. May it be long ahead of you." He took one last look into Cedric's sapphire eyes before walking out.

    The Witch's sweet smile stretched wide as she watched Cedric examine his father's sword. Forged by the Mother Tree herself and gifted to the Winter King when he was chosen, no other being could wield it. The blade would simply turn back to ice and melt if it fell into the wrong hands, but in the hands of a true Winter Guardian, it was a formidable weapon, stronger than any steel and never dulled. Cedric was on the edge of tears, trying to understand all at once the importance of what was happening.

Winter's Heir

The sword in his hands was heavy with the weight of the past, his past, and his future.

"Drink your tea, Guardian. It will help you sleep. I think it's time you got to know your other half."

Chapter Twelve

The inside of the Winter Guardian's home was very different from the Witch's. The fireplace was the same, but a flame hadn't been kindled in it in many years, the cold remains of burnt wood and ashes still sitting in the hearth. A large bed sat against the far wall, covered in gray and white furs. A huge archway opened the back to the outside, large enough for Snow Bringer to enter or leave as needed. The beast lay on a bed of old hay on the floor and turned to look as the Witch and Cedric entered. Cea'um Two'um whinnied deeply at the sight of Cedric, and the man felt an odd chilled rush fall over him.

"He is happy to see you; can you feel it?"

"I feel cold, is that him?"

"Yes, you can feel his emotions, and he yours. He is your Companion, and you are his Guardian. Neither is above the other, but rather equals, two parts of the same whole." She walked over to the bed and ran her fingers through the soft furs, tossing small clouds of dust into the air. "This is the Winter Guardian's second home, no other may enter without your permission. You will find your father didn't own many possessions, but there may be a few things still here. Do you need me to light the fire for you?"

"I think I can manage. Thank you, Witch." Cedric approached and sat at the end of the bed beside Snow Bringer's head. She nodded slightly before turning to leave.

"Get as much sleep as you can; it will be the last chance you have to get a full rest in until we reach Spring Meadows." Snow Bringer whinnied again as if to say, 'we will be fine,' and the Witch left the home to return to her own.

Even though the straw under them was kissed with frost, Cedric did not feel the chill. It felt like the cold was almost a part of him now, and his breath steamed in the warm forest air. Instead, he felt like he was overheating, like he was standing too close to the fireplace even though it hadn't even been lit. He pushed his hand into Snow Bringer's mane and found he was thankful for how cold it was. The Beast's ears perked up, and an image flashed in front of Cedric's vision. It was the ancient script, curling and twirling into a word and all at once he knew it's meaning, felt it in his soul. Garuk. Come.

Cedric crawled closer until he was leaning against Snow Bringer's chest, and Cea'em Two'um wrapped his neck and head over Cedric's shoulder as if cuddled for warmth, but the opposite was true. The chill from the Companion's skin cooled Cedric down, and he sighed comfortably. He gently patted the muscular neck before closing his eyes, ready for sleep to overwhelm him. Tomorrow a whole new adventure lay in front of him, and he knew he was one step closer to the beautiful maiden of this dreams.

His eyes flitted open and Cedric stood knee deep in a snowdrift, flakes of white twisting and twirling around him as the frigid wind pulled and pushed them around. Before him was a vision of Snow Bringer, decorated in ornate frozen plate armor, and gray-white furs. A huge man sat upon him as if prepared for war, a snowy beard draped over a thick chest plate with an image of a rearing Snow Bringer and a cowering beast he had never seen before displayed in light blue. A crown of jagged ice shards circled the king's head, his sapphire eyes peering through Cedric as if he weren't there. Cedric could see a Tar'una wolf inching quietly closer from the rear just out of the sight of his father, growing bolder and snarling as it moved towards the king, keeping close to the ground.

That was when his father dismounted from Snow Bringer and said in a deep grunt, "I am Frost Slayer, and you will obey me!"

With a quickness that Cedric had never seen before, the Winter King's sword was drawn, then deep into the heart of the massive wolf that had tried to sneak behind him and made its move. It howled in agony before falling limp off the ice sword.

The other wolf lay and showed his belly, giving in to the new alpha of his pack.

The vision twisted and contorted, and Cedric found himself suddenly in an open prairie, tall, golden grass flowing up to his chest. Again, he could see his father, but now he walked beside a woman, tall and slender with light-bronze skin and long, fiery hair. Her red dress hugged her hips and swollen belly as she moved and faded into orange as it dragged behind her. A golden crown sat lightly on her head, moving in the late evening light as if it were an open flame, flowing and flickering.

"I wish to birth here in my own lands, in the warmth of Summer." Her voice was as smooth and sweet as nectar as she turned to Frost Slayer to gauge his reaction.

"What? Why the change so suddenly? Everything is already prepared at the stronghold; your midwives here would not be prepared for—"

"It is what I want, husband," she said sternly. They stopped, and the Winter King looked deep into her golden eyes, taking her hands into his and slowly kneeling before her.

"If it is what you wish, my love, then it shall be done. Whatever the cost." He leaned forward and put his forehead on her swollen belly, and the queen ran her fingers through his white hair. "You are my everything, Ember. Until the Mother Tree takes back my soul, it belongs to you."

Chapter Thirteen

The sharp prick of a pin jabbed into King Korva's side, causing him to let out a furious "uuff!" as he looked down at the small, red-haired woman with a mouthful of pins hanging from her lips.

"That's the last time, Risha. You are not competent enough for a seamstress. Go back to the kitchens where you belong!" he barked at the small girl as she ran out of the room, tears streaming down her face but knowing what would happen if she angered the king any more.

He turned and looked at himself in the full-length mirror. Curly, tangled, brown hair sat roughly under the golden crown that never fit his head quite right no matter how he had tried to force it down. The red with gold-trim wedding suit he'd had made for him was now just a bit too tight, the decorative buttons down the front stretching in their holes to contain his larger chest. He knew it wasn't the girl's fault the attire no longer fit. Too many feasts and festivals had made him over-eat, but he couldn't help himself from lashing out at her. His rage grew harder and harder to control, and he found pleasure in fewer things as the days went by.

He had thought that having control of all Da'nu would appease the darkness inside of him, but the more he claimed under his flag, the more it fueled the desire. The mountain of coins and jewels he had collected from his subjects used to bring a smile to his face, but still the overwhelming need to have more would creep in, and even all their shine and brilliance couldn't stop it.

The red-hot anger drained from his face as his thoughts turned to the image of Colla

Tep'um, that beautiful fair-haired maiden of Spring Meadows. Her long, sun-kissed, blonde hair that always smelled like roses, her gentle, kind, gray eyes, her sweet mouth as it glided into a smile…

"She will make me happy again, Dar E'um. I know she will."

Against the far corner of the room, almost blending into the red and gold stones, the massive thorny head of Sun Riser rose off the worn floor. His blood-red eyes lazily opened and glared at the man.

"She is so beautiful, Beast… and that golden hair! I must have her as my bride."

The dragon snorted out a puff of smoke as if to laugh and shook his head before resting it back onto the stones.

Korva's face heated again as rage overtook any happiness he had found. He turned quickly to face Sun Riser.

"Do not mock me, you filthy animal!"

Dar E'um lumbered to his feet, thick, clear, crystal nails clicking against the hard stone. He pulled his head high to look down at the king, the tips of his black rock horns almost brushing the cathedral ceilings. Massive leathery wings stretched out to fill the room. He puffed up his chest and blew a streak of liquid fire in front of Korva. The light danced across Sun Riser's scales, the streaks of gold along his sides shining brightly, and cast glittering shadows against the ceiling.

"You do not scare me, Beast; have you forgotten who I am?!" Korva thundered out before taking a deep breath. Thick, black fog poured from the man's open mouth. It billowed and piled, rolling over the fire and extinguishing it with a hiss before pooled around the dragon's feet. Tendrils crawled up his legs like wispy vines, wrapping around his chest and up his long neck until it found his nose. Sun Riser's eyes quickly filled with fear at what he saw in the fog, and he backed off his show of force. With a sharp howl, he crawled as far into the corner as he could, covering his face with his wings and shaking with fright.

The corners of Korva's lips curled up in a satisfied smile and his eyes glowed dark red, the darkness if his soul quenched for the time being.

"I will have her, Sun Riser. She is an object just like anything else. I will own her because I want her, just like anything else."

Chapter Fourteen

People crowded the camp as the sun dipped below the trees. Snow Bringer and Cedric stood waiting as countless masses came up to shake hands or pray to the Mother for their safe journey. A jet-black horse of normal stature stood next to them, the steed the Gypsy had chosen for the trek. Past her, a few had decided that they wished to go on the quest with them, and they lined up neatly, waiting to begin. Each steed was packed with tents, food, and anything else each believed they would need in the coming weeks.

Among them was Jar'ra, a quiet but optimistic woman with brown hair and muddy eyes who was one of the camp's healers. Sephr, a tall man in a thick, dark cloak that Cedric recognized, he always sat outside his tent, cleaning and sharpening his vast dagger and sword collection. And lastly, three short men with a white horse, a peculiar bunch. The Witch had told Cedric that they had once been one man, but after a bad illness almost killed him, he had made the journey to the Mother Tree, and She had split him into three to save his life. It sounded like a rumor, but he could never tell with the Witch's stories. They all had a blue tint to them like they had had trouble breathing for a long time. Their veins puffed out across their skin like they were desperate for air.

A small girl in a ragged, brown cloak shuffled up to Cedric, her violet eyes staring at the ground as she approached.

"You prob-ly don't know who I am, Guardian of the Winterlands, but you did know my mama…" Cedric went down on one knee to get a better look at the child. Her black hair was tangled and shoved behind her ears, but one look at her eyes and he knew.

"Your mother was Naria, wasn't she?"

"Yes, sir. Now both Mama and Papa were taken by the beasties." Dread filled Cedric, his ignorance that morning had made this girl an orphan, a dangerous thing to be in this world. "She was a weaver, made all the clothes and tents for the camp." She held out a dirty hand and opened it to show Cedric a small gold chain with a circle locket hanging from it. "She gave me dis when I was just a babe, she said it was lucky. I want you ta have it. You need more luck than I've ever gotten from it." Cedric gently picked up the necklace and held it tight, unsure of what to say but a small "thank you" slipped out of his throat. He turned to look at the Gypsy Witch, who watched the discussion intently.

"Coo'ara, have you been practicing and reading your book?" she spoke tenderly to the girl.

"Yes'um. It's a bit hard to read, but I'm gettin' through it. I'll tell you 'bout it when you get back." The Witch nodded and stared at her feet for a moment.

"Just keep reading and talk to the Wind. She knows all your woes, child." The girl nodded and turned, walking back into the crowd without another word, leaving Cedric to rise and face the Witch, his hands fumbling with the small clasp. She took it from him and expertly hooked the necklace around his neck.

"Thus, starts your Kra."

"Kra?"

"All Guardians carry with them a necklace or chain with charms, some gifted and others collected. All hold power or memories from your travels and accomplishments in Da'nu. We live very, very long lives, and it is a nice reminder to have your world hanging from your neck. Come now, it is time to begin."

Snow Bringer bowed as Cedric pulled himself onto the slim, leather saddle he had found at the Winter Guardian's home. Bags and bundles were strapped to the back, and his father's sword hung from a loop on the side.

The Witch gracefully swung onto her horse who pranced impatiently, followed by the healer and the cloaked man onto their bay horses. After some time and a lot of grunting and shoving, the three small men finally got settled onto their horse. The crowd hushed as the realness of the moment set in for them.

Ahead of them was the dense second ring of the forest, a broken archway, and a small stone wall marking the path. The Hunter was on his Stag in the passageway and yelled out to the crowd.

"Stay within the camp, and you will be safe. Stay inside in the day, light your fires at night, and you will be safe. Do not lose faith in the power of the Mother."

They turned, and Snow Bringer slowly followed, the rest close behind.

Chapter Fifteen

The sickly sweet smell of death wafted through the air in waves as they slowly moved down the overgrown path deeper into the forest. The black fog grew thick around their feet, making it impossible to stay on track without the Hunter leading them. Out of the corner of Cedric's eye, he could have sworn he could see glowing red eyes staring at him through the black trunks, but every time he looked, nothing was there. If it weren't for the cold that had settled into his heart, the night chill would have had him shivering, like the others that had joined them.

"It's almost beautiful, in an 'everything here wants to eat you' kind of way," Jar'ra whispered as she rubbed her hands together, her breath fogging in a thick cloud. In the deafening silence, her voice carried like a yell and even the equal beat of the falling hooves was swallowed by the fog.

"Pretty empty for how dangerous you've made it seem, Hunter," Sephr mumbled out deeply. The Hunter didn't even acknowledge the man's words, just kept steadily moving forward, adjusting their path to take the clearest way.

The outer branches of the Mother Tree, and the closeness of the forest around them cast out all light the moon would have given off, only the extremely faint purple glow given by the fog gave any way to see in front of them at all.

The three dwarves had fallen asleep, leaning on each other as their white horse plodded along at the back of the group. Time dragged by painfully slow, each step forward feeling hours ahead of the last. Twisted trunks and knotty branches looming over them, stretching down as if they would grab the group up at any moment. Cedric remembered the old stories about the trees here being able to move on their own, and a small shiver ran down his spine at the thought of bark and boughs twisting around his chest. He wasn't the kind of person that showed his fear, but he could feel it. A rising tension in the pit of his stomach that he couldn't shake.

The Stag stopped so suddenly Snow Bringer's snout bumped into his rear. The horses' ears perked up and turned, hearing something humans could not.

"What is it, Hunter?" The Witch urged her horse forward to stand next to the Stag.

"They've never nested here before; this path should have..." a hair-splitting scream interrupted him, so close that Cedric's ears rang loudly as he tried to put his hands tightly over them to block some of it out.

"Run! Everyone run! Screamers!" The Hunter pulled the bow off his shoulders and docked an arrow. The bay horses scattered into the woods. The white horse reared, throwing one of the dwarves to the ground before taking off as well.

A bloody claw swiped in front of Cedric's face out of the darkness, catching his shoulder and tearing the fabric of his shirt. Dark fur with sickly yellow spots hung from the knuckles, exposing the decaying gray muscle underneath the torn rotting skin. Blood-red, cat-like eyes locked onto Cedric, contracting as it focused onto him and the hairs on the back of his neck stood straight up. The twisted creature's mouth was stuffed with rows of chiseled sharp teeth, glowing green drool dripped off its cracked, bleeding lips. Hot, sticky breath billowed over Cedric in a toxic cloud, reminding him of a battlefield after a week in the sun. The stench twisted his stomach painfully, but his muscles seized in fear as he stared into the face of the Screamer.

Snow Bringer pulled hard against the reins, pulling them from Cedric's frozen grip and took off at a full gallop, weaving and bobbing between the trees. Cedric dared not look back, even as the human scream of pain and terror rose behind him. He buried his face into the frozen mane and let Snow Bringer go wherever he felt he needed to.

The creature had been massive, the open paw at least as big as Cedric's head. Even with the weeks of training the Hunter had put him through, nothing had prepared him for the sheer size of the beast. The image of its face burned into his memory, the smell still trapped in his nose. It shook his resolve, and he finally understood why the Hunter had worked him until he dropped every day.

He suddenly realized the Hunter had docked an arrow before Snow Bringer had bolted, and he should have stayed and fought with him. Cedric felt cowardly running away like he had and contemplated turning back, but the fear that still held a grip on his body prevented him from doing anything.

Snow Bringer slowed into a canter, then a trot. He breathed heavily from the escape, and Cedric picked up the reins to pull back softly and bring the six-legged horse back to a walk. He had no idea where they were, other than lost and alone in the Forest of All, with the faint rays of the morning sun starting to lighten the hopeless landscape around him.

Chapter Sixteen

The arrow flew through the muggy air for an instant before embedding itself down to the feathers in the right eye of the Screamer, who was feasting on the body of the dwarf that had fallen in the initial attack. It let out a guttural yowl, bits of fabric and skin stuck in its teeth and blood mingled with its glowing drool. Breaking the shaft of the arrow with its paw, it turned its wrath to the Hunter and the Gypsy. The shriek was deafening, even the Mighty Stag pulling against the Hunter in an attempt to run to safety, but they held steady and faced the beast, pawing at the dirt and snorting loudly. The Witch pulled her staff from the bundles behind her and jumped from her horse, who took the opportunity to flee into the woods.

She landed hard into the fog and jammed the thin end of the staff down in front of her, impacting the ground. A burst of energy flowed out from the staff in an amber light, forcing back the haze and knocking the Screamer onto its back in a cloud of dust. The Hunter pulled another arrow from his quiver, docked it, and let it fly with one swift motion. It found its target in the other eye, completely blinding the huge beast. It recovered from its fall and stumbled around furiously, swiping with immense paws at where it thought it could hear the Witch and the Stag. The Witch ran straight for it, staff in both hands in front of her. She swung the weight of the blunt end around before twisting it up over her head and bashing the dirt with all her strength.

Thick, brown vines emerged from the soil, pushing up and twisting around the Screamer's legs. The final swipe of a free paw dragged one claw across her shoulder, searing into her skin and causing her to yelp in pain and fall to her knees. The vines rapidly grew and engulfed the Screamer, twisting tightly around its body like snakes. The beast let out one last screech as the vines covered its head, trapping it in overgrowth. Buds of orange grew from a few spots in the vines, bloating and expanding until they were about to break before slowing down.

"Are you all right, enchantress?" The Hunter rode over to the Witch and dismounted, pulling her up and into his arms.

"I will be fine, Brave Hunter. It's a flesh wound, it will heal. We must find the others." Crimson blood trailed down her sleeve as she spoke.

"Yes, we must. It's almost daybreak and that one was the mother, her kits should be around here somewhere. If we do not find them and kill them before they get hungry, their cries will call the alpha male, and it will only get worse as the sun rises if we don't make a secure camp." Instead of letting him go, the Gypsy held tighter to the Hunter.

"I do love you, Guardian of the Forest," she whispered to him.

"I know, my sweet Autumn Witch." He lifted her up and placed her gently onto the Stag's saddle. "I will find the kits. You take the Stag and see if you can find somewhere we can rest safely for the day." He picked up her staff from where it had fallen and slipped it into the straps of the bundles behind her.

"The river should be close by. If we are still on the same path, I may know of a comfy place."

Chapter Seventeen

Fear bubbled up from his gut, but he pushed it down. Cedric knew what he had to do. The sun was rising, and if he didn't get a decent camp going with a high fire, the beasts would come.

"It's just building a camp, you've done this hundreds of times. Army training," he reassured himself. Undoing the straps holding down the bundles, he dismounted. One held a tent and sleeping sack, another food and a pot, and the third held the flint stones, clothes, and a few things he had taken from the Winter King's home.

Cedric looked around at the lifeless forest as the sun tried its best to break through the shadows. Where light did speckle through the dense intertwined canopy, it burned away little pinholes in the thick fog that surrounded Cedric's feet. Daylight meant the creatures would be hunting soon. A nervous rattle shook his bones at the thought of what else was living between the crooked trunks and dried bushes. If he could build a big enough fire, they would stay back.

    Between the patches of dead grass and the flint he had brought, it was easy enough to turn a spark into a fire, and with a whole forest of seasoned wood around him, keeping it going wouldn't be a problem either. As the fire grew, the fog rolled away, exposing the dry and cracked earth around his campsite. Thick, white smoke billowed out from the bonfire Cedric had made, rising through the forest like a huge moving tower.

    He stopped for a moment to examine his work before setting up his tent. Short, wooden poles with interlocking bases had been expertly carved and bent to make two arches when connected, each about five feet tall. The fabric was light and strong, woven carefully with skillful hands. Loops on the sides showed him where to position the poles, and the tent rose into place. He stood back to admire his work, and thanked Naria under his breath for her expert weaving, wondering if she ever knew her work would be relied upon so heavily for safety. He traced the small painted symbol of " " on the top of the tent before stepping back to admire his work.

It wasn't much, but it was a secure camp with a tall enough fire that the beasties would stay away.

He moved the other two bundles and the sleeping sack into the tent when he heard Snow Bringer whinny. He jumped out of the shelter expecting trouble, but the huge horse didn't seem scared, just attentive of the figures moving towards them. Out of the fog, Jar'ra and Sephr on their bay horses had seen Cedric's smoke and rode to it.

"I'm glad someone had the right mind to make a camp," Sephr said coldly as they entered the circle.

"Well, I knew someone would. That's why I said we needed to look." Jar'ra sighed lightly, "You build a strong camp, Guardian."

"Thank you, Jar'ra. At least the army taught me something useful for out here."

"At least King Korva's army taught you anything at all," Sephr spat out under his breath. He had already dismounted to set up his space, exactly opposite the circle from Cedric's.

"He's just grumpy because he didn't get to kill anything. Have you seen the Hunter and the Witch yet?" She dismounted with a thud, her thick leather boots kicking up dust.

"Not yet, I fled too. I think one of the dwarves is dead." The scream of pain behind him as he rode away still fresh in his mind.

She nodded as she unstrapped her bundles from the saddle.

"Help me set up my tent, and I'll make us a tea to sleep through the day. Try to find them tomorrow."

Chapter Eighteen

"I'm telling you, ten crystals are more than enough payment for one day in a damp cave." The Gypsy stood her ground with a handful of shimmering, clear lumps. A fairy, no more than a foot tall, stood in the entrance way, one glittering blue hand rested on his hip, the other held tightly to an arrow with the flight feathers torn out. He wore animal hair crudely woven into a loincloth, and small, sharp teeth hung around his neck and wrists. Glistening dust fell from his four, fragile, iridescent wings as they twitched impatiently.

"No can do, miss. No pay, no cave."

"Damned sprite, it's daytime and you are denying a Guardian of a safe place to rest."

"That may mean something to you, miss, but this deep in the woods? We own this cave. No pay, no cave."

The Witch sighed deeply. Fairies were a tricky bunch, but they didn't lie. Usually, they were a lot more helpful, but if not they were typically attracted to shiny things. This one, however, seemed to be completely unphased by the glistening stones in her hand.

"What do you need to be paid in Faye?"

"Preferably? Meat. Blood. That sort of thing, but at this point, just about any dead thing will do nicely." He picked at his teeth boredly with a pointed nail, pulling out a small tuft of fur that had been stuck there for some time and flicked it off onto the stone.

The Witch pinched the bridge of her nose against the headache forming between her eyes.

The forest and its inhabitants had changed so much from what she remembered.

"This should be more than enough for the day then?" The Hunter's deep voice boomed as he approached from behind, each hand held five limp Screamer kits by the tails. They weren't as decayed as the mother had been, but their small bodies were still unmistakably Screamers.

"Are those fresh?" the fairy asked hungrily, licking his lips and wringing his hands.

"Still warm." When he was next to the Witch, the Hunter dropped all but one of the dead animals. He threw it onto the flat stone in front of the fairy.

The shiny, blue being couldn't contain himself, and he pounced onto the cat-like beast. His teeth tore through the thick hide like razors, his tongue making sure to get every scrap of meat that clung to the bones. Soon, the whole stone and carcass were covered in a layer of blue dust, and the fairy was bathed in blood. He eyed the nine others at the Hunter's feet, chewing on the liver.

"What does his grace want for the others?"

"Five for a few days in the cave, and the others for a bottle of your Shimmer." The Hunter crossed his arms, showing that his offer was firm. The fairy stopped chewing for a moment.

"That's potent stuff, Your Grace; not for the faint of heart." Bits of meat fell from his mouth as he spoke.

"It's not for me. Do we have a deal or not?" The fairy mulled over it for a moment, but the taste of meat and the promise of more won out in his mind.

"Fine. Deal. Yes. Take the cave. It's got a nasty leak in the back, unfixable!" He flew up and around to look the Hunter in the eye. "Leave your bottle by the food; it will be filled by dark time." And he buzzed off into the forest.

"Damned sprites," the Gypsy spoke when she knew he was far enough off not to hear her. "Selling my own cave back to me."

"Once the Faye pick a territory, it's almost impossible to convince them to leave, and I haven't come here enough to protect it." He unpacked the Mighty Stag, throwing the bundles onto his shoulders like they weighed close to nothing.

"How long has it been, Brave Hunter?"

"Since when, Sweet Witch?"

"Since the trees here turned black, since the fog has infected more than just the animals?"

She looked around at the space that had once been lush and well cared for, her heart tightening at the sight. The path up to the dark archway that was once carefully lined with delicate flowers was now overgrown with dry, thorny weeds. The moss covering for the entrance had been left to grow on its own, no longer the trimmed and pruned curtain the Witch had spent so much time on in the past. Even the stone steps that had formed from years of bare feet walking up and down were discolored and covered in dirt and dust.

"Two and a half decades."

"It doesn't feel like it could have possibly been that long. But I believe it." She walked up the three or four steep steps, over the bloody mess of cleaned bones and blue dust, and into the spacious, cool cave.

Chapter Nineteen

When the white horse finally made it into the circle around Cedric's campsite, it was drenched in sweat. Bloodshot eyes looked around wildly, every moment of the fog against the black trees looked like another monster to the poor animal. Thorns and bits of branches clung to it's mane, and its face was covered in small scratches. It pranced around, snorting and snuffing, trying its best to keep all four hooves off the ground at the same time.

Cedric rushed to try and grab onto the wild-eyed animal, Snow Bringer blocking from behind so it wouldn't run into the fog again. It took some time, but they finally calmed him down and got the dwarves, supplies, and saddle off.

"Come now," Jar'ra's caring voice soothingly hushed the two dwarves. "I'll make some tea, and we can all get some sleep and forget this."

"There's no tea that can make them forget this." Sephr felt like he needed to chime in.

"You want to bet on that? I brought my whole kit. I could make you forget your mother if I needed to." She shot him a hot, angry glare, daring him to say anything more.

"I need to get—"

"—to the Mother," the dwarves shuddered out. Cedric noticed their skin was even more sickly than it was at the camp, and it was starting to become scaled in spots. They were taller now too, bringing them up to about midway on Jar'ra's side, their pants now squeezing tightly and stopping just below their knees. Cedric caught himself staring at them and quickly turned away to start unpacking their tent.

"And we'll get there, but we must rest for the day and try to find the Hunter and the Gypsy when night falls." Jar'ra huddled the dwarves in a blanket she had brought out, almost like a mother bird cuddles her young under her when it rains. She sat them down next to the fire and ran into her tent to grab her kit.

She returned on quick feet, holding a rolled blue leather case, with a white cross on the back, and a green leaf painted through the center. With a flick of her hand, the case was unrolled onto the ground. Small, glass vials, each with their own pocket and filled with many different powders, were lined in perfect tight rows. She took the ones for sleep, memory, and calm. Taking small fabric pouches and a tiny metal measuring scoop from a pocket on the case, she measured out individual combinations into the pouches.

"I'm assuming you don't want any tea, Sephr?"

"No, you can keep your strange powders to yourself." And he turned and went into his tent.

Jar'ra measured out the memory powder, just half a scoop into two of the bags, then a full scoop of sleep and calm for each. She was tying them closed when the big black kettle nestled at the edge of the bonfire hooted to life. She lifted it off the coals with a leather glove.

"I'm hoping everyone packed a cup?"

***

The Hunter struck a fire to life on a small pile of twigs and weeds in the back of the cave while the Gypsy swept dried leaves out the opening with an old knotty broom. The Stag lay just outside, his antlers covering the gaping hole. The way the sun bled through the trees made the Stag's fur look like bark and his antlers branches. Any passerby would have thought a tree had fallen over the opening of the cave.

Inside, a small, simple, wooden table sat against the wall, covered in a thick film of dust. A candle that had long been extinguished was a pillar for cobwebs at the center of the table. Shelves had been carved out of the gray rock, and small painted trinkets sat at attention on their ledges.

As the fire crept to life with crackles and pops, the Hunter stood and unraveled his sleeping sack. The Gypsy, satisfied with her work, let the broom lean on a wall and unpacked hers as well.

"I miss the old days, Hunter. Do you remember when we would sneak away and meet here?"

"I do, Sweet Witch."

"When all we had to woe over in this world was whether you dried your socks after swimming." The Hunter chuckled to himself as he pulled off his cloth shirt. The Gypsy's eyes danced over his toned chest and countless scars, smiling to herself.

"One time. I forget to do something one time in fifty years."

"And never will I ever let you live it down."

The Witch loosened the front of her corset, and the Hunter loosened the back for her, a simple dance they had done a thousand times before, though it had been some time. He kissed her softly on the side of her neck, inhaling her rich pumpkin and roasted apple smell.

"Oh stop, I must smell horrible." She giggled and danced away from him.

"Never, you have always smelled like a perfect day in Autumn Fall. Now let me see your shoulder. I saw the Screamer caught you."

The Gypsy slid her torn sleeve off her shoulder, the thick gash obviously more than a flesh wound.

"It will heal, I'll be fine."

"You need to stop lying to me, Gypsy." The Hunter went over to his bundles and hurriedly pulled out a red canvas bag. "This time, your lie may have killed you."

"Nonsense. It doesn't burn like the one from the battle."

"Screamers are different, Gust Runner." His tone had darkened considerably, a cold seriousness settling onto his face. He used her given name like a parent uses the full name of a child. "Screamers have green saliva from the numerous bacteria that live in their mouths. When they lick their paws after a meal, their claws become covered in the bacteria." He pulled strips of white fabric, a needle, a small bundle of frosty, white horse hair, a block of wood, and a bottle of green leaves with blue dots down the center.

"Which is why Ember died from her wounds." The Hunter took the leaves from the bottle and tore them up, rolling them in his palms before pressing them lightly into the gash. The Gypsy winced as the pressure flared the pain to life, hot streaks raced down to her fingertips.

"You'll want to sit for this part, my love." He threaded the needle with the white horse hair.

Chapter Twenty

Settling against the frozen back of Snow Bringer who had lain in front of the entrance of his tent, Cedric pulled a parcel of letters and drawings from his bundles. He had found them in a small wooden chest under the tall bed at the Winter Guardian's home, and his curiosity wouldn't let him just leave them alone. He hadn't had the time to go through them, but as he unpacked his sleep sack, he remembered he had wrapped them in his clothes.

He carefully pulled the wide, frosty ribbon and the frozen bow fell open freely, like it was meant only for his hands. The first was a letter by itself, handwritten with dark ink on paper made of pressed yellow petals.

To Frost Slayer,

Winter's Heir

I write to you this day to speak of the incident that occurred during our last meeting in Guardian Grove. I am most embarrassed by my actions, far too much mead on a warm night without anything to eat. I was being far to forward, and I feel the need to thank you. You are a proud and strong man for taking me back to my home when I had far too many drinks to do so myself. If you ever find yourself getting lonely in that frozen fortress to the north, don't hesitate to call on me. I would very much enjoy the idea of spending more time with you.

Until we meet again,

Ember.

Cedric's heart dropped into his gut. In his hands, he held letters from his mother that his father had kept safe in a box under his bed. He traced her gentle, waving signature across the bottom of the paper. This was before they were married, before Korva had tried to destroy the Mother Tree.

"This was how they met," he whispered to himself, paging slowly through the pile. The papers were all different colors, each made with a different flower or material. Her flowing, curly handwriting decorated each one with care as their love grew over the years. He wondered if he and Petal would have letters like this one day. He thought about writing one now when Snow Bringer huffed from outside the tent, grabbing Cedric's attention away from the love letters.

"Cedric. It's your watch, I need some sleep," Sephr quietly called from outside. Snow Bringer stood and walked off while Cedric quickly put the letter back into the stack and retied the ribbon around it. Before he could put it back onto his bundles, the ribbon froze into an icy band around the treasure that it was meant to protect. He smiled and grabbed his father's sword.

"I'm awake, Sephr. Give me just a moment."

***

The sun had begun to set again before the Gypsy awoke, the Hunter sitting against the wall of the archway, staring outside through the Stag's antlers.

"You overslept your watch." His voice was low and grumbled from not having said anything for most of the day. The Gypsy went to push herself off the sleeping mat when her shoulder felt like it had been shoved into a fire. She yelped as it gave out, but the Hunter gently picked her up and pulled her to standing.

"That was a joke, I'm sorry. Please try to not use your shoulder."

"I will be fine, I just need time to heal," she said stubbornly.

"And it won't heal if you keep moving it. I'll have to make a sling for you." He went over to his supplies.

"No. No one else must know." He stopped what he was doing and looked at the Gypsy, her hazel eyes locked with his emerald ones. It was a tense moment before she spoke again.

"If Cedric and the others find out I am hurt, they will want to abandon the quest," she calmly explained. "We don't have time to turn back. The king plans to marry Colla Tep'um at the end of the month, at the start of the Spring Festivals. If we keep moving, we can make it before that and have a chance at setting things right again."

"It will be suicide."

"And letting Korva destroy Da'nu without even an attempt to stop him is somehow not?" She tried her best to cross her arms, but after her shoulder shouted in pain and an involuntary hiss escaped her lips, she settled on putting her hands on her hips and staring the Hunter down. "This is something I must do. When we get to the Mother, I will ask if she will heal me, but if things are as bad as I see them to be, she will be growing weak in this fog."

"Just promise me you will not bullhead your way through this. That cut could kill you if you ignore it."

"You tell me these things like I do not already know them." She walked over to her pile of clothes and grabbed her belt of satchels with her good arm. "I have treated more wounds from these beasts than the whole rest of Da'nu." She pulled a pinch of golden dust from one of the small sacks and sprinkled it into their fire. It rose with the smoke out of a small hole in the back of the cave. "I held Leo'ra's hand as she bled out with two new babies to brood over."

They said nothing as she dressed, he helped her tie up her corset and gently kissed the back of her neck.

"I don't want anything to happen to you, my love, not while you are in my care. You are the only thing in my heart, my soul would be lost in the darkness without the light of yours to guide it." The Gypsy smiled softly at his words.

Chapter Twenty-One

As day crept into night, Cedric took slow, steady steps around the circle of his campsite, the icy sword strapped tightly to his waist. A path wore into the dry earth where Jar'ra and Sephr had walked the same route earlier in the day. He watched as the shadows grew long and the fog rolled in where the sun could no longer reach. Bands of light stretched out across the dense forest, painting a twisted maze of light and fog.

Cedric stopped in his tracks as soon as he saw them. In the thorny thicket, not too far from where his protective circle ended, two red eyes blinked. They weren't as large as the Screamer, but the feeling of dread at seeing the violent shade staring at him had him wanting to run back to his tent.

His hand grabbed the hilt of the sword out of trained instinct, and the creature stepped out into the light.

Its face looked almost human. The shape and placement were right, but the nose had completely decayed off, leaving just the holes in the bone where the nose should be. Its mouth was so full of uneven layers of paper thin, jagged teeth, it couldn't close its jaw properly. The skin looked like it would shed off with the smallest touch, so thin in places, one could see the veins trying to push thick blood through lifeless limbs. Extended, crooked toes stiffly supported its weight as it paced in the band of light with almost bird-like movements. Its back was arched almost completely in half near the neck, leaving the head to cock to one side in order for it to see in front of it. Useless arms were tucked in close in obviously painful positions, the claw-like fingers going in every direction.

Cedric's body took a step back, fear riding up his spine as he tried to run.

Snow Bringer planted his hooves and caught Cedric against his chest, frost flowing from his mane as he lowered his neck over Cedric's shoulder.

"*I am Frost Slayer, and you will obey me!*"

The voice of the Winter King echoed up from his heart, and his eyes shone in a deeper, more brilliant sapphire. He could feel the power and confidence his father had been known for fill him, and he locked eyes with the beast.

"I am Cedric, Guardian of the Winterlands, and you will obey me." Now calm and collected, he pulled the sword from his side, the flawless clear blade softly humming as it left the frozen sheath. A blanket of frost grew from Cedric's feet, dividing the fog and showing the way to the beast. He ran straight for it with no hesitation, sword at the ready.

He had just enough time to breathe in before the blade dove into the chest of the warped animal, stopping only when the hilt reached the skin. Cedric stood firm as he collided, pulling the blade up as hard as he could. The perfect, icy edge separated the two halves of the terrifying face with almost no resistance.

"Wow," Jar'ra uttered from behind the flap of her tent. She watched as the decaying body of the beast tried to gurgle a cry before falling limply to the ground, the icy path quickly consumed with crimson. Cedric stood, icy sword held straight to the sky in shaking hands when the sun finally set under the trees and threw the landscape into a twilight. A chorus full of howls, screams, cackles, and hoots filled the dimming air with an eerie song. The fog filled the voids in slow waves, caressing every tree and bush until it was everywhere again.

Jar'ra slowly emerged, engrossed in the cacophony around them. The bonfire was now the only source of light, but just under the canopy of interwoven branches, something shone. She looked harder, but she wasn't too sure of what she saw.

"Cedric, do you see that?"

Her soft voice behind him brought him back to himself, and he lowered the sword. He looked back at her, then off into the forest where she pointed. At first, he didn't see anything, but she was right. Something reflected light, flashing and glittering through the wall of crooked trees. As he moved to the side and craned his neck, he could almost see it.

"It looks like… golden smoke?"

"That must be the Gypsy Witch. Maybe she and the Hunter stayed together. We should head that way as soon as we get everyone awake and break camp."

Cedric nodded and looked back at the bloody mess of animal he had taken on.

"That was pretty impressive, Guardian. I don't think I've ever seen anyone move that fast."

"I don't know what came over me."

"Courage. True raw courage, and it was marvelous."

He nodded softly, Jar'ra went to wake Sephr and tell him what she had seen. Cedric cleaned his sword with the edge of his tunic before sheathing it and waking the dwarves.

Chapter Twenty-Two

"Oh good, they saw it!" The Witch sighed in relief, leaning out of the cave entrance as Jar'ra and Sephr, followed by the dwarves and Cedric, plodded along towards the Gypsy's cave. They held torches to scare away the fog as they followed the twinkling through the trees.

"Like ants holding sparks. It will take them half the night to even get here, and it takes a full night and day to cross the river and get to the next shelter."

"So, we will stay here for an extra day. Or go off the path, that shortcut you and I built."

"Gypsy, that bridge hasn't been touched in over twenty-five years. Who knows if it could hold the weight of a bird let alone horses and people."

"It will save us a day of walking and trying to go across the river in a boat that most likely can't even hold water."

"If we go off the path, we could stumble into another nest. What if we wake up a Sprinter? Or a Spitter?"

"Sprinters have never gone to the far side of the river—the water holds them back. Spitters are tree nesters; so long as we keep with the plan of night travel, we won't disturb them. It's our only real option, Hunter."

"It's a dangerous one." The Hunter stood at the table, a hand-drawn but detailed map with yellowed, cracked, curling edges laid across the freshly dusted wood. He hated to admit when she was right, but if they went all the way to the old boat crossing, it may not even be there anymore and they would lose even more time, possibly a day or even two as they tried to find or make a different way across. "I will ride down to the bridge. If it looks stable enough to cross, we will take it. If not we will have to try the boat. I should be back before they get here."

***

Jar'ra and Sephr rode in front, setting the pace as they quietly weaved through trees that grew wider as they went. The fog that had been just tall enough to creep on the ground like snakes was now high enough to cover the horses' knees. The fire they carried could do almost nothing to hold it back. Every step they took, the slow, black waves on the side of the path rode higher and higher. But they followed the golden smoke like a beacon in the dark night, each step careful and well placed.

"Fallen log," Sephr called behind to warn the dwarves and Cedric, stopping once his horse was over.

"Oh Mother, Sephr, look." Jar'ra pointed just past him at the end of the fire's reach. Soft, black fur laid in a mangled mess, white bones showing through.

"Looks like the Gypsy's horse. Must have tried to jump in the fog and landed badly." Sephr carefully dismounted and walked over to what remained of the beautiful, black horse, the fog high enough to reach his waist but the fire from the torch kept it at bay.

Something had torn into its belly and its throat had been ripped out. All manner of prints had walked through the puddle of blood, smearing and tracking it across the dry dirt. Both front legs had broken, leaving the animal defenseless and immobile, easy prey for the warped predators that stalked the forest.

"You think the Gypsy—"

"—is all right?" The identical dwarves looked pale and almost green in the strange light. A small amount of blood dripped from one of their noses but was quickly wiped away with a brown cloth.

"I think the Gypsy is fine; that golden signal fire is uniquely hers. All those tracks there and not one of them looks human. Cedric, is there room on Snow Bringer for more supplies?" Jar'ra dismounted too, walked over to the carcass, and unknotted the Gypsy's bundles from the gnawed-on saddle.

"I should be able to strap them on here. If she is safe at the end of the golden smoke, she will be happy to have a change of clothes, I'm sure."

"And her food. I guess evil doesn't like salted pork and dried fruit strips." Sephr handed Cedric the bound possessions, still stained with splatters of dried horse blood. As he pulled them up, Cedric noticed a vine made of bronze wrapped around the woven sacks, keeping them tightly secured.

"Now, Sephr, they aren't really evil; they know not what they do."

"Honestly, Jar'ra, how you can look at a scene like this and somehow not see the complete brutality of it, is beyond my abilities."

"I like to think that maybe I have a larger understanding of the world than you." She released the last pack and threw it at Sephr, who caught it with a strained grunt.

Dried leaves rustled together high in the trees above them, and everyone froze. Speckles of brown and black leaf bits slowly rained down on the group. All eyes drifted up. Broken branches had been carried and carefully interlaced high on the tree's peeling bark until it had made a thick nest that tied the neighboring trees into a gnarly mess, one that at present had a family of Spitters trying to sleep in it.

"Now look what you did," Sephr harshly whispered at Jar'ra.

A smooth, scaly head poked out over the side of the nest, eyeing them intently with red slit eyes speckled with gray. It let out a noise somewhere between a coo and a cackle, tilting its head to try and see past the light of the torches. A tense moment passed. Glowing eyes blinked twice. Its long snout opened wide in a lazy yawn, fangs longer than Cedric's hand extending for a moment before retracting against the spitters jaw as it closed its mouth. It puffed up a fan on the back of it's neck and cackled again, a bit lower this time. A warning before shuffling back into the nest. No one moved. They could hear at least five more Spitters chirping and chipping in protest at the one that was trying to get comfortable again. More branches and leaves fell before the family settled down, leaving the forest to its eerie silence. Cedric counted to fifty before letting out the breathe he hadn't realized he was holding.

"We have to go. Quiet as you can before anything else knows we're here." Cedric pointed at the glittering, golden column that rose just over the next hill. The two nodded in agreement and worked silently, getting the last bundle up to Cedric and remounted their own horses. With a little gentle nudging, the tired bay horses,

Winter's Heir

Snow Bringer, and the dwarves' white horse moved deliberately and carefully down the path.

Chapter Twenty-Three

Korva sat on a polished black-stone throne, his hand tightly gripping the deeply carved arm of the chair and frustration twisting his face. Sun Riser lay behind him, curled around the throne and his head resting on the end of his tail. A lone man stood shaking before his king, a scroll with a broken wax seal held tightly in his sweaty hands.

"How long ago?"

"We just received word this morning, but the messenger said he has been riding hard for almost three weeks, Your Grace."

"They have been invading Autumn Fall for three weeks without a captain? I doubt they've conquered anything at all." He pinched the bridge of his nose, trying to contain his urge to strangle the man for giving him bad news. "Who was the deserter?"

"Cedric Youngmoore, The Knight of Darkness, Your Grace."

"Now that genuinely shocks me. Of all my knights currently serving, he was the most determined to please. Did the messenger mention why?"

"No, sire. He said he was in mid-sentence when he just turned and ran."

"Odd, very odd. Was he chased at least?"

"For a time, but the search party couldn't stay on his trail. He is very cunning …" The man's voice trailed off and dissolved into squeaks as Korva rose from the daunting throne.

"Spend close to two decades training someone only to have them stab you in the back. I'll have to send a new knight to replace him, after the Spring Festival. I don't have the men to spare until then. Have we received any word from the Spring Queen?"

"Not as of yet, Your Highness. She has neither accepted nor denied your request."

"She will, no one denies me. As beautiful as she is, she will see the advantage of joining me. If not, I will have a large enough troop with me, it would be easy enough to persuade her through force." His face and hands grew hot as anger bubbled to the surface.

"You plan to force her hand?" the man stuttered out, his very bones shaking in fear as Korva stepped over the dragon's tail and slowly circled him.

"I don't plan on it, no, but if she refuses to do so willingly, she doesn't leave me much choice. I will have her, either beside me on the throne or in her own room in the prison." Korva had never even considered that the beautiful Petal Dancer wouldn't swoon to be at his side. He was wealthy and powerful beyond measure, and both of their kingdoms would benefit greatly from the joining. But it had been close to a month since he had sent his proposal, and she had yet to respond. He slowly walked around the man, the darkness rising within him like molten rock bubbling up from the deep as he fought to squash the doubt. "She will. She must."

The man, desperate to change the subject to something that wouldn't get him killed, brought up the Borderlands barrier, the army that could move that way, and the reports for the morning. Korva heard none of it, and eventually dismissed the man just so he could have silence to think. He ran out of the room like he was being chased, and the stone doors closed behind him with a resounding thud.

Korva was left with his echoing thoughts in the spacious hall, alone except for the sleeping mountain around the throne.

"How could she not want me? I have everything..." He dropped to his knees, the too-small golden crown falling from his head and loudly clattering against the cold, dark stone. His chest ached, and he wheezed. His breath turned dark, and he coughed up the fog. It poured from his eyes like thick, wispy tears as he struggled to wipe them away. His hacking and choking bounced around the hall in waves, and Sun Riser opened his heavy eyes.

Winter's Heir

Fog twisted around Korva like a storm, billowing and swelling around him until it completely enveloped him.

"Why would she want to take you as her husband? She knows what you've done. She hates you!" The voice was slick and seemed to come from all around Korva. He tried to look for the source, but his eyes couldn't make out anything. His body felt heavy and slow like he was underwater.

"I have everything she could want, and she is everything I want. She could make me happy for the rest of my life!" He yelled out into the rolling darkness as he breathed normally again, but his lungs were full of the thick fog, and he had to inhale deeply to not go unconscious.

"You don't feel happiness. All you feel is Greed and Anger. It has eaten you from the inside, and there is almost nothing left of you."

"No. I am Korva, King and Guardian of Summer and Winter." He pulled himself off the floor. The voice coldly laughed.

"You are no Guardian. You are no one. You are just an angry little child who's still mad that Mommy took away your toys."

"They were your toys, not mine!" Korva tried to find somewhere to direct his anger, but nothing was there. It boiled inside of him until he shook.

"You didn't even bond with the winter beast, he refused you. You tricked the dragon, he would refuse you if he had a choice. And now, you're going to get upset when you are confronted with the thought of a real Guardian

rejecting you? You understand you murdered them, don't you?"

"Silence! I demand silence!"

"Is the truth too scary for you, Korva?" A form grew from the fog, gentle, flowing, golden hair laid on delicate, pale shoulders, a dress of white flowers hugging her hips and stopping as it touched the ground.

"Petal Dancer?" He reached out his trembling hand to touch her shoulder. He could feel the calm pull her beautiful body brought him, and he wanted that, more than he could breathe.

Her shining hair twirled as she turned to face him, perfect glee painted on her face like a soft melody that melted his heart into his feet. But she stopped. Their eyes made contact, and she stopped, seeing who he was. Her beautiful face dropped into confusion, then fear, and finally disgust before she backed away from him.

"No, Petal, it's me! It's Korva! Please!" he begged, clutching his chest as it tightened around his breaking heart. She picked up her sparkling, pure flower dress and ran, tears streaming down her face.

"Please make it stop." He fell to his knees again; his arms were weak, and he felt like his soul was shattered. His lungs burned as they fought for air. "Please, I can't take this anymore."

"I will break you, over, and over, and over again until you are numb. Only then will you be worthy to be king of anything."

Chapter Twenty-Four

A wave of relief washed over Cedric when they came upon the entrance to the cave, and the Gypsy Witch stood there. After seeing her horse like it was, he almost jumped off Snow Bringer in excitement.

"You had me so worried you know, running off like that," she jokingly scolded the group as they walked into the clearing. The trees had been clear cut from this spot many years ago, only the proud stumps remained to dot the hillside. The moonlight was so clear it could hold back the fog here, but small lanterns hung at the tree line and along the stone path to mark the safe area. Crude stone steps led up to an old archway cut into the hill, the cave inside gently glowing from the fire within.

"Your horse fell—"

"It didn't make it." The dwarves helped each other off as Jar'ra and Sephr dismounted.

"You won't believe what I saw!" Jar'ra piped in.

"I still don't," Sephr muttered.

"Calm down. There will be time for all of us to talk, but we have to keep moving tonight. You made good time, so we do have a moment where we can eat, but we need to cross the bridge as soon as we are able. There is an old prayer village, just inside the third ring that will be a safe space to stop, and we can save time." She looked up at Cedric, a sadness hiding in her face. "The bridge will be the most perilous part. It hangs low to the river, and we will have to pass through the fog. The bridge itself is solid and passable; as long as we don't let our fears get the better of us, it should be a rather uneventful crossing,"

"I brought my whole kit, Gypsy."

"Oh good, that will be helpful. The Hunter has a surprise for you, don't let me forget."

"Did you get everyone gifts or just her?" Sephr crossed his arms under his dark cape.

"Sephr, you've always been crabby, but that borders on rude."

"He's just mad he wasn't the first to kill something." Jar'ra unknotted two rolls from her saddle and carried them up to the cave.

"I didn't see it. I didn't hear it. It didn't happen."

"Oh, it happened. Your ego's so big you can't see past it."

"That's enough. Grab your food and get up to the cave. You two bicker like an old married couple." Sephr grabbed the dwarves' and his bundles from the horses and walked up the path. Cedric unknotted the top bags from Snow Bringer.

"Witch, I have a lot I need to ask you." He thought about the pile of letters he had stashed in his clothes, the moment of courage against whatever it was at their fire yesterday, about his father's voice rising up inside of him...

"I will do the best I can over lunch, but most will have to wait until we are at the prayer village."

"We did get your things." He pulled the neat rolls wrapped in copper cord off and handed them down to her, but she didn't grab them.

"Hold, Cedric. I will get her things." The Hunter's voice almost made him jump. He was suddenly right next to the Witch, grabbing her sacks and loading them on his broad shoulders.

"Thank you. Now come on, we must prepare for the crossing."

As the group softly munched on the leathery fruit strips and overly salty pork, Jar'ra had unrolled her kit across the table and the Witch and she leaned over it, picking individual powders and quietly conversing about the best matches. Sephr and the Hunter had chosen to sit in the entrance, looking out over the dark forest and pointing at the hand-drawn map in the Hunter's hands. Even the dwarves sat together, as close to the fire as they could get without burning themselves.

Cedric stood in the middle of the overly crowded, overly hot room, the red and blue strips of dried fruit looking completely inedible in his hands. He knew he had to eat, but between the heat and his racing thoughts, his stomach had screwed in uncomfortable knots.

"So we're ready then?" the Gypsy's voice broke through the chatter. All heads turned to her. Jar'ra and the Hunter nodded.

"The thing we are about to pass through—the fog—it is a living thing. A vapor made of particles of darkness. As you pass over the bridge, over the River of Tears, you will go through the lowest point in the Forest of All. It's all uphill after the river. As you inhale the particles, they collect in the brain. Slowly over time, you can see troubled breathing and dementia. Long-term exposure causes blood to pool in the eyes, loss of oxygen to the skin, causing it to gangrene and rot... All the animals you see have lived in the fog for twenty-five years or were born in it.

"We will not stay in it long enough to see any of the side effects. At most, twenty minutes, and we should be high enough on the other side to relight the torches. In that twenty minutes, the particles will rush to your brain and learn your darkest fear. You must stay in control of that fear, or it will gain control of you."

Chapter Twenty-Five

The Hunter took his torch and lit a brazier that sat just from the start of the path to the bridge. Within seconds, another and then another lit up with a silver light that lined the overgrown but dead path, although each grew dimmer the deeper into the dark fog they looked.

The path down to the bridge was lined with lanterns, burning bright with glittering silver light. It was worn and clear, despite having not been touched since Korva's betrayal, and wide enough for the horses to make it through easily. Cedric could hear the sound of crashing water as the bridge came into view. Everyone stopped and dismounted. Two huge trees stood on the edge of a cliff, their branches were long and stretched across the divide where it met more branches in the middle from trees on the other side, forming the bridge. It hung low over the rushing water, the fog completely covering most of the bridge. The Witch was the first to break the silence they had traveled in.

"Before you is the River of Tears. The great and powerful waterway that passes through the roots of the Mother and out to the rest of Da'nu. The only source is the melting ice from the Winter mountains, so the water is very cold. The roots of these trees are thick and strong, trust they will hold. We will send the animals across, then we will pass." The Stag, the two bay horses, the white horse, and Snow Bringer were all led through the trees and walked across the bridge alone, the fog covering them as they made their way. Cedric watched as Snow

Bringer calmly disappeared below the thick, rolling blanket, fear threatening to choke him.

"All right. Now us." The Hunter walked out onto the stretched roots. His torch washed out with a hiss, and he walked the rest of the way, bathed in darkness.

The dwarves were next, then Cedric. He stood between the two trees and looked out over the edge. He felt a hand on his shoulder and turned to see Jar'ra, handing him one of the tea bags with a rainbow of powders in it.

"If it gets too much to handle, this can help you get through it. Just inhale this and keep walking. I'll be right behind you," she whispered over his shoulder and walked off.

Cedric closed the small fabric bag in his fist, held his torch high, and took a deep breath.

His face felt hot, and Cedric realized he had been closing his eyes. The sun blinded him for a moment, but birds chirping cheerfully from the tree line made him open them. The root and branches bridge had been patiently twisted and tied to make a wide, continuous path that sank low over the sparkling river. Fairies sat on the twisting branches, their glittery wings dropping dust into the wind.

"I have been watching you for a long time, Cedric. It's so good to have you here," a voice echoed out like it was right over his shoulder, but nothing was there. "You have power locked deep inside of you. I can help you bring it out."

"No, I just want to get across this bridge." Cedric took a few confused steps.

"Please, Cedric stay awhile. There's so much I've wanted to show you."

Winter's Heir

The miraculous scene in front of him bent and swelled, and he grabbed onto the branches to keep his balance. The fog was all around him, and it was dark again. The bridge was old and creaked as it moved, the roots and branches black and overgrown. The waterfall thundered in his ear, but it was dull and without life.

"You remember your father, don't you?"

The fog in front of him shimmered, and a man stood on the bridge. He was tall, looming over Cedric with dark-brown hair and eyes, an exact image of the man who raised him. He held a whip in his hand, and his face looked down in front of Cedric in disappointment. He was looking at a girl, her own long, brown hair covered her face, but Cedric recognized her with a pit of dread in his chest.

"No, Papa, please. It wasn't me!" *Young Tea-ala lay in a ball at her father's feet. Her thin cotton shirt already torn and stained with red.*

"You speak out of line again, you're going to feel it, girl!" Cedric took a step forward, and his father pointed at him with the whip. "Are you wanting one too, boy?" his father said as he cracked the whip across Cedric's right arm, and the realness of the sting surprised him.

"I can make all of it better and help you change what that man has done to you. You can save your sister from his anger."

"Everything I grew up with has molded me into what I am today, no matter how harsh it was."

"You will bend one way or another. Just like Korva fell to my call, so shall you."

"You are nothing but particles. I am Cedric, Guardian of the Winterlands!" He pushed himself forward, stumbling through the images in the fog, and he watched them dissolve into the murky air around him.

"I am Darkness and all that encompasses. You are a man, weak and without purpose." The voice was deeper now, and it emphasized its irritation with Cedric. "I can give you that purpose. All the strength you would ever need."

"Strength is nothing without courage." A few more steps before the background twisted again, and even though the bridge held stable, it had Cedric reaching for the sides.

A familiar voice called out as the fog settled, "Get back in line, you filthy dung bug!"

Cedric stood fast, and although he knew it was just a vision, years of training had him *falling back in line. It was the first day Cedric had joined the king's army. He had been so terrified that day, he hadn't noticed anything around him. Cedric could see now, off to the side, King Korva whispering into one of his general's ears. That general nodded, and he walked down the line of boys that stood shoulder to shoulder, stopping at Cedric.*

"You boy, have been picked by the king to earn your rank in the arena games."

"I was there this day. Korva didn't think you would make it far. I told him you were full of fear of being sent home and would do anything to prove your worth."

Chapter Twenty-Six

Korva sat up suddenly, realizing the voice that had kept him locked away in his own thoughts for the past thirty years had vanished. The aftermath of a burst of thunder shook the glass in his window. He looked around his room, nothing had moved since he fell asleep, but it sounded different. He could hear the workers in the kitchen clattering dishes a few floors down, the maids laughing as they dusted rooms. He could hear a horse in the stables, the pitter-patter of rain against his window… He felt like he could hear everything. First, a smile crept onto his face, then tears welled up in his eyes as he realized everything that had happened.

"Where did it all go wrong?" The harder he tried to connect the dots the farther apart they seemed. Memory after memory flooded him, but nothing was clear. Until a memory more solid then stone hit him square in the chest. He was breathless for a moment, and stars flew in front of his eyes.

The stars sparkled in complicated designs, covering the clear sky. The blanket under his head was soft and smelled like fresh roses, and he could feel something warm in his hand.

"The night sky is so beautiful this time of year." The beautiful, sweet voice he had dreamed about whispered into his ear. Petal Dancer squeezed his hand, and he could feel the warmth of her happiness wash over him. He knew this moment, better than any other. His stomach was full of flitter bugs all over again. She rolled to look at his face, and he turned and

looked at hers. He watched in awe as her eyes sparkled and a wide smile spread across her face at seeing him. "I love you, Korva. More than there are stars in the sky to count."

"I will love you forever, Petal Dancer, until there are no more stars to count." He could feel the words form and fall from his mouth, and he could feel his heart throb against its cage. He tried to hang on to every moment of the memory, the sound of crickets, the smell of clover and roses, but his joy and calm sharply ceased as he heard the deep, slithery voice.

***

"You were born with me in your blood. You fought under my flag. You had a purpose because I gave it to you."

"No. I love her." Cedric's voice had grown weak, and exhaustion made his arms shake as he tried to hold onto the bridge.

"YOU love her? You've never even met her!" The fog shifted, and Cedric was on his knees at the foot of a hill covered in sweet grass and wildflowers. The night sky unrolled over him, the pure number of stars giving enough light to see the silhouette of two people lying at the top.

"But I have met her. At the Spring Festival."

"An exchange of glances is not love. A woman of her standing could never love you. You are darkness, Cedric. Stay with me and I will show you."

Korva felt helpless as he sat on the hill, gazing into the stunning eyes of his love. The fog didn't know he was here, in this memory, and it had someone with him. The name was familiar like he knew it well but couldn't place from where.

Petal Dancer sat up, grabbing Korva's hands and pulling him up too.

"I had always pictured this moment to be special." She blushed slightly, and a few strands of her golden hair fell over her face. Korva watched as his hand gently pushed them back behind her ear, the tips of his fingertips brushing her soft skin. He almost cried from the memory of the sensation.

"Every second of every day is special when you are here, my love."

"You never loved her, and she will never love you."

Korva ripped against the memory, and every inch of his skin fired off in pain.

"That's not true!" Korva yelled, then stood at the top of the hill. The scene continued to play behind him. "I have loved her since the moment we locked eyes as children. I courted her for centuries until we were old enough to declare our love. She was my everything, I molded the inner gardens to show my love for her! Please!" He saw Cedric, and realization ran cold in his veins. "Youngmoore? Cedric Youngmoore?"

Korva took off full speed for Cedric. He slammed hard into his shoulder.

"You must believe what I have to show you."

They were now standing on their feet at the far edge of the river, but the fog was nowhere in sight. "I was on my way back from the Mother with the crown of blossoms for my love. But my Stag bucked me off, surprised by a snake that had curled on the trail."

"Why should I care about anything you have to say, Korva?"

"Just watch, please," he pleaded. "I don't know if I will ever get a chance to tell someone again."

Leaves rustled, and a stick cracking behind Cedric had him turn. A glorious white Stag with gently curving antlers almost pranced down the green path, head held high. A young Korva with brown, curly hair and light-emerald eyes sat proudly on its back, his hands gently holding a crown made from many white flowers.

"I fell into the rushing water. I can't swim, and the water was so cold, I was unable to grab onto anything. It pulled me too deep."

Cedric watched as the other Korva was bucked from his Stag, and into the water below. Korva was drowning, holding his neck and twisting in the water, the last bubbles of air slipping away from him and spiraling to the surface. He watched as the motion of the waterfall sucked him down.

"I didn't know what to do, Cedric. I was so full of fear, fear of losing my love, fear of not being able to help the Mother Tree in the creation of our precious world. Out of fear, I used my gift to create something to try to save my life."

Now he could see Korva reaching for the sky with both arms. He could see that, even though he was underwater, he was screaming and shaking, not from the cold but from pure fear. Cedric watched as Korva's hands molded the water around and into his palms as it changed from the crystal clear of the river into the black evil that was the fog.

"This is not meant for you, Cedric." The fog hissed from the other side of the river, anger growing within the fog, weakening Cedric once more, causing him to fall back to a knee.

He watched as the ball of fog that Korva had created, slithered into his mouth, changing his eyes from a light emerald into red, then a black emptiness.

"Please, Cedric... Please, you have to help me."

The swirling mass on the other side yelled at Korva and Cedric.

"There is nothing that you can do to stop what has been started! You will join me, Cedric, and I will have what I want!"

With a hard thud and pressure on Cedric's back, he fell forwards. He could hear Korva pleading with him, and the last thing he could hear was his voice, thin and echoing through the darkness. "If you don't believe what I have shown you... Find the crown. Find th—"

Winter's Heir

Chapter Twenty-Seven

Jar'ra fell on top of Cedric, her hands reaching out to catch herself but only succeeded in pushing Cedric into the dirt on the far side of the river. She immediately jumped up and grabbed him by his shirt, pulling him the last few feet onto firm land. He was breathing, but he wasn't moving, and his eyes were glossed over. She fumbled with a pouch on her pants and took out a small strip of fragile, almost clear paper. She wrapped it around the top of her torch until only the very end was in her hand. She put it on the palm of her thumb and snapped.

Brilliant, silver light tore Cedric back to reality. He breathed in so hard, he thought his ribs would break, his whole body desperate for the clean air. He pushed off the ground, and Jar'ra pulled him up so he could stand. The Hunter grabbed his arm to help him steady himself.

"Breathe, Cedric. Come back to us."

"I'm here, Hunter." Cedric's eyes adjusted to the bright light of the torch, and he could see who had made it across the bridge. The dwarves sat on their horse to stay above the fog, and the Stag, Snow Bringer, and the two bays grazed on the green grass of the hill. The Hunter held him up, and Jar'ra looked him over as worry evaporated from her face.

"You didn't even take the powder, did you? I told you, courage!"

"Who is coming across next?" the Hunter asked Jar'ra.

"I think it was Sephr, then the Gypsy." He nodded at her answer.

"There's enough of us over. If you want to go ahead to the prayer camp, you should be safe. I'll meet you there once they make it safely. Follow the stone trail up the hill, you won't pass it."

***

"The prayer camps were built as an easy path to follow for missionaries to reach the Mother," Jar'ra explained to Cedric as they steadily went up on a natural flat-stone path. The fog was left behind at the river, and the third ring of the Forest of All lay before them. This was land that had always grown under the protection of the Mother's branches, and as Cedric looked up over the trees, he could see them with real clarity for the first time. Rising from the hill, her brown bark was adeptly curved and formed ancient words in the grooves. Her strong arms wove around each other in complicated patterns, all reaching for the sky. A ring of dark, starry night could be seen where the blanket of her branches ended but before the shadowy, dead forest began.

"She's unbelievable."

"She is everything, Guardian." Jar'ra pointed up at her trunk, at one of the symbols that faced out over them.

"You see that one there? That is 'Air,' or 'Coo.' See the way it swirls at the top, then drags into a zig-zag?" Cedric could see the pattern she described, but he was so stunned with the beauty around them as they slowly climbed the hill, he didn't notice that Jar'ra had pulled her bay to a halt. Snow Bringer stopped a few paces more, and Cedric realized they had reached the prayer camp.

It looked like at one time it had been a well-used, well-kept campsite, but after so long of being left to the elements, nature had reclaimed the circle. Large boulders still jutted from the outer edge, struggling to hold back the thick, green tree line. A smaller circle of stones sat in the middle, but moss had almost completely grown over it, making it look like just a lump in the ground. Trees had been planted in front of the boulders and weaved into a canopy overhead, leaving a hole in the middle over the fire ring, though they had grown unruly in their time alone and unkempt. It was large enough to fit all the tents underneath.

Jar'ra dismounted with a gentle thump on the soft ground, and it brought Cedric back to himself.

"Did someone build all this?" he asked.

"Some of the old stories say that the first Guardians and their Companions, the Stags, did when they were creating Da'nu." Jar'ra unpacked her supplies, moving them under the canopy, so Cedric did too. "Others say one man built it as a way to travel from the Tree to his love, and then when it was used as a prayer walk, it was lined with rocks and tended to by all who chose the path." They helped each other set up tents and get a decent fire going. Before long, the Stag and the other bay came up to the camp, and they all dismounted, placing their tents in the circle under the trees.

Chapter Twenty-Eight

Cedric sat in front of his tent, looking out over the forest when the sun rose into the ring of sky he could see. The Gypsy and the Hunter had just finished setting up their sleeping spaces, Jar'ra and the dwarves had already fallen asleep. He had so much information fighting for attention, his head hurt. Was what Korva showed him true? Was it all just a show put on by the fog? He felt like it had taken him days to cross the bridge, had it really only been twenty minutes like the Witch had said before they crossed?

"I'm guessing you want to talk." The Gypsy stood next to him, holding two cups of tea. He had been so consumed in the sunrise, he hadn't even heard her kettle.

Cedric had already explained everything that had happened on the bridge up to when Korva yelled at the fog. He began to explain everything he had seen while on the riverside as the Hunter who had been leaning on a root that stuck up curling beside his tent, took a seat next to him asking, "Korva was there?"

"He was more than there… He pulled me out for a moment. I felt him as he grabbed my shoulder, I felt his voice when he screamed at the fog…"

"It may have all been an illusion."

"But what if it's all true? Did Korva love Petal Dancer?"

"I remember when we were children, he was infatuated with her, but we weren't very close as we grew."

"Then what if we've had it wrong all these years?" The Gypsy stood and slowly paced around the fire. "We assumed the darkness inside of him had been there since he was born, an eternal thing. But this... if it is true, that means the darkness is a creation. What has been created can also be destroyed."

"Without proof, there is very little to say that it wasn't just a trick of the fog."

"He asked me to help him. To find the crown he had been carrying that day."

"If he was going to give the crown to Petal, he would have dropped it on the Spring side of the forest. Along the prayer path."

"Then it is settled," the Hunter said with almost disbelief they even considered any of this. "The Witch and I will leave at daybreak for the bridge to Spring and see what we can find. If what you say is true, the crown should be somewhere around there."

"While we are gone, you and the others will need to pray at the altar. We are going to need all the help we can get, and you, Cedric, must receive your armor from the roots of the Mother."

***

Cedric's sleeping sack had never felt so comfortable, but his reeling mind kept him just from the edge of comfortable sleep. He heard Snow Bringer nicker from the other side of the tent fabric, and the word flashed in his head.

Garuk. Come.

He sighed deeply and pulled himself up and out of the fabric dome. Snow Bringer stood behind his tent; his chilling presence had frozen the ground, covering it with a fuzz of frost.

"What does it all mean? Did I even love her at all? Why did I ever leave my post? I must love her. I can feel it in my chest when I think about her," he rambled, not entirely sure if he expected an answer from the six-legged shaggy snow beast that stood staring at him. "I have questions that I don't know who to ask. Is King Korva the rightful man to claim her hand? What is my purpose?"

Snow Bringer sagged his head and knelt before lying on the ground.

Garuk.

Cedric walked over and sat so his back was against the animal's chest. He felt a cooling wave of comfort wash over him as he leaned against the thick fur. Small snowflakes gently drifted from Snow Bringer's mane, settling on his shoulder. Cedric yawned deeply, the exhaustion taking over.

"I have to help him."

Chapter Twenty-Nine

Jar'ra, Sephr, the two dwarves, and Cedric had disassembled their tents and buried the fire. The Gypsy Witch and the Hunter left on the Stag maybe an hour before, as the sun made its descent through the ring of sky.

"The fog really got to you, didn't it?" Jar'ra asked as she helped him fold the fabric. Cedric stayed quiet, not wanting her to know the kind of horror he had grown up in. "You don't have to tell me about it. I know how painful the past can be. That's why I became a healer."

"What do you know of pain?" He could still feel the stripe from his father's whip the fog had given him across his arm, a phantom reminder of the hundreds he had received on his back when he was a child.

"What do I know... you better watch yourself, boy." She held one of the wood poles she had been rolling into the fabric out like a wand. "All my scars are on the inside."

"Boy, you're no older than I!" he roared but caught himself. "I'm... I'm sorry, I meant no disrespect. Maybe I did, but I've been so confused." Jar'ra's face softened, and she lowered the pole, rolling it up into the fabric and tying it shut.

"The fog can do that for certain people. Causes irritability, frustration, loss of sleep, memory loss..." She threw the last bundle onto her bay. "Just off the path here, is the altar. When this path was used as a prayer trail, those who dedicated their life to worship would come to these altars to leave gifts for the Mother."

The old stone blocks that stood around the Altar of the Mother were moss covered and wind beaten, showing their age with ancient beauty. Giant gold and orange leaves, large enough that they could be used as a tent, lay on the ground in front of the decorated archway. One drifted lazily through the air before landing weightlessly just off the path. The dense, vibrant jungle forest took on a whole new life in the moonlight. Broad leaves unfolded over the day plants, decorated with bright dots, swirls, and lines, glowing with their own amber light. Flowers opened along the rocks and out of cracks, trimmed with yellows and golds. Even the vines that hung low between the trees seemed to glow, and there was so much light around, there was no need for torches.

A root had come through the earth, thick and twisting, and had unraveled to show the pure, clear waters that it carried before diving back into the dirt. The water flowed like a miniature river through the root, and Cedric stood in awe of how blue it was.

"The Tears of the Mother, or the Blood of Da'nu, depending on whom you ask," Jar'ra announced. "The wishing roots are said to have been around since before the Companions, and it gave them their power as Da'nu was forming." She walked over to the root. "These waters feed all of Autumn Fall, the fruit trees, the animals, everything. Like an underground river system. Tradition holds that you must leave a gift for the waters to ensure a safe journey up the hill.

"If you buy into all that crap," Sephr muttered from back on the trail.

"It's scientific! You can follow roots all the way to the far reaches of Autumn to the Borderlands. But you wouldn't know that, as you've never been out of the Hunter's Camp."

"Lies! I made it over the bridge, same as you! Same as him!" He flicked his cape and mounted his bay. Cedric thought for a moment he could see red in his eyes, but it was gone before he could think it was anything other than a trick of the light.

"Oh, go on and be a grump then. We'll meet you at the Temple, and you better be cooled off when we get there."

Sephr nudged his bay on with an angry huff and rode off up the stone trail.

"I'm sorry about that. He's been a real pain since last night." Jar'ra shook the tension out of her hands that had been clenched into fists, her stone bracelets rattling.

"Since the bridge?"

"Yes. He's not himself…" She started to explain but trailed off, a pained look contorting her face as she turned her attention back to the root. "It became known as a wishing root as missionaries would drop their gift of coin into the waters, with the wish of bringing wealth to the land." She pulled at the tie around a small, beaded sack at her waist and pulled out six small, silver circles. "Written scrolls from the last attempt to reach the Mother speak of the water's healing properties, especially for animals. Her power has run through this land since the first turn of the sun."

"Last attempt?" Cedric questioned. "How long has it been since anyone has walked this path?"

"The last successful quest was the day before the Great Betrayal. Most attempts after that never made it over the bridge. The last was almost ten years ago. A giant hiding from the prosecution of his lands under their king took five men and a notebook and made it as far into the forest as he could." She glanced softly at the dwarves sleeping on the white horse and dropped the coins into the water.

Chapter Thirty

Korva's world slowly slid back to his bedroom, sparks of light fading out into the dark, lavish room. He hung onto every detail he could manage to catch, from the sound of the rain tip-tapping on the glass windows to the look of the fuzzy, velvet curtains.

Because he knew what was coming, he wasn't ready to go into the darkness, and he still didn't completely understand how he had gotten here. The last clear memory he had was drowning in the river. He could remember feelings, some colors, but it was like the fog had taken them, leaving just a blur where the memories should be.

A flash of Petal Dancer, her golden hair shimmering in the moonlight, lying on the blanket looking at the stars.

"My love..." he whispered as the storm at his window calmed. "I'll make it right. I promise." His emerald eyes shone softly as the last flash of lightning lit up the room and softly glowed for moments after. He let the thunder wash over him. It rumbled in his soul, and his heart beat hard in his chest. He knew he couldn't stand against the darkness, not alone. He knew it would be coming back soon, and he would be locked into the dark hell he had lived in since that day at the river, but for the first time since he had watched the black fog crawl into his mouth, he knew there was a way.

The overly decorated bedroom lit up as the first ray of the rising sun broke through the thunderclouds, the intense summer heat forcing them to dissipate. Everything seemed to be gilded in shining gold, casting the light around in odd designs. What wasn't gold was crushed red velvet or polished, black stone, and Korva swallowed hard against the tears forming. As they turned back into the deep black, as they had been for the last thirty years, Korva closed his tired eyes, pulled on the sound of the Stag's hooves against the packed earth, and let himself fall into the darkness.

***

"You hold hate in your heart. You shall not pass." Snow Bringer's ears swiveled towards an unknown voice, and Cedric pulled back softly on the reins.

"Hate in my heart? There's about to be hate in my hand as I slice you down." Cedric recognized Sephr's voice and noticed what he was arguing with on the path.

"Oh, that's not good," Jar'ra whispered from behind him.

Its body was cat-like, stocky legs sat on wide paws and supported a muscular chest, but the fur shifted into feathers as they went up the neck and crested over a bird-like head. Huge, heavy feather wings rested on its back, falling open as it became bored with the human's attitude. It sat taller than Snow Bringer and towered over Sephr and his bay. Every inch of feather and fur, down to the creature's smooth beak and twitching tail, was stone gray and looked like the small rocks that lined the path.

"A Drum'ma." Jar'ra slowly dismounted and just watched.

"Only those pure of heart and mind may pass. You are not pure of either, I can smell the hate in your heart. Now go, you are not welcome on this path."

"You don't scare me, rock bird. I've been wanting to kill something since the first night in this lost place, and if it happens to be you, so be it." Sephr pulled two long daggers from his waist and held them up like he would throw them.

"Save your blades, human. It will only serve to make me forcibly remove you. I have stood since I was called from the earth, I will stand long after you are called back to it."

"Enough, Sephr! Has your anger blinded you so much that you don't see what you are threatening?" Jar'ra yelled and stepped forward, drawing the Drum'ma's attention.

"A whole group of humans! What a strange day this has been." The beast leaned past the bay to get a better look.

"A Companion and his Guardian! You forgot to mention you were traveling with anyone." It stood up straighter and puffed out its chest, pulling the heavy solid stone wings up in an impressive display of power. "Halt, all ye who travel here! Only those pure of heart may continue on this path." It seemed to hold itself like it had waited a long time and practiced many times, just so it could say that one bit.

"Well, at least you got it right that time, stupid rock bird."

"Human, if you offend me once more, I may feel the urge to eat you, and that would be bad for all of us. Hate doesn't digest well." The Drum'ma glowered at Sephr, who finally decided to just keep quiet.

Snow Bringer and Cedric plodded forward, right up to the stone beast. It looked them over with clouded, quartz eyes, and Cedric realized it probably couldn't see very well, if at all.

"I feel the power of the Mother in you, but it has not yet seen its full potential. I can smell the darkness on you, but it is faint. You have carried it a long time. I don't believe we've met, human, though I know your Companion well."

"I am Cedric, son of Frost and Ember."

"So you are, born of fire and ice, but you take after your father. Such a mighty hero was he! You will find your purpose, Guardian of the Winterlands, just keep following the path." The Drum'ma pulled in its wings, and Snow Bringer carried on, Cedric glancing behind at Jar'ra and the others as they went.

"What the fark. He passes your mystical test but I'm not good enough."

"Sephr, please…"

"No! I will not calm down! Every one of you thinks I'm not good enough! You'll see, I'll show you I'm ten times the man that boy is!" He pulled roughly on the reins to turn his bay into the glowing woods and kicked it hard in the sides, and it took off with a scared leap. They bounded through the thick jungle until they were out of sight.

"Step closer, so that I may get a whiff of you," the beast spoke to Jar'ra, and she led her horse by the reins who in turn led the dwarves who were still sound asleep, slumped in the saddle of their white horse. The Drum'ma bobbed its head, sniffing the air around Jar'ra and her bay.

"I feel the power of the Mother in you, but it is faint and asleep. I smell no darkness on you, and the purity of your heart is blinding. The answers you seek are along this path. You may pass."

Chapter Thirty-One

The path wove its way up the hill, winding and twisting around the overgrowth. They walked on even as the warm morning sun stretched out over the land, until it was high in the sky and hiding behind the arms of the Mother.

"We must be getting close," Cedric mumbled after yet another sharp turn around a tree. It felt like they had been going for days, and even Snow Bringer's head slumped as they went.

"We are, just a bit farther, and we can make camp at the Temple." Jar'ra yawned and readjusted herself in the saddle, realizing her legs had grown numb from being still for so long.

"How do you know all this stuff anyway? You're no older than I."

"My parents were the record keepers, history hunters. Our home was always full of old scrolls they had saved from the latest exploration, drawings and maps of where they were headed next... They weren't home most of the time. I lived in those scrolls and played out the adventures when they were gone. We lived in a little house at the edge of Summer before it touched the forest. I can still smell the garden and almost feel the paint chipping off the fence."

"So, how did you end up at the Hunter's Camp?"

"My parents had left to find some lost tablets from the first century, but months later, they hadn't returned. The Gypsy Witch came and moved me to the camp, just until my parents returned. That was about eight years ago." She looked down at her hands as they fiddled with the reins.

"I'm sorry..." Cedric wasn't sure what to say, knowing the topic must be a sore spot for her.

"I'll find them one day. That's why I volunteered to go to the Mother Tree, to find them. She will have the answers."

"I hope so." Cedric looked up over the trees at the colossal being that was grounded at the center of their world. Sunlight seemed to trickle from her branches down her trunk, riding the creases in her folded bark and bringing a glowing light to the plants that lived in her shadow. Vines with orange and red flowers draped through the trees, all leaning up the hill to face the Mother. At her base, a simple stone temple stood as a testament to time. Parts of the walls had crumbled away, but a proud bronze archway rose in defiance, soaking up the light and shining like a beacon at the top of the hill.

"Now we're almost there." Jar'ra softly smiled.

***

"Mother, I must be getting old." The Gypsy Witch yawned as the Stag came to a stop at the river bank on the Spring side of the tree. The Stag breathed deeply and thankful to stop, going to its knees before lying down.

"Old? You are as stunning as the day you were chosen." The Hunter descended from the Mighty Stag. "The sands of time have done nothing against your faultless form."

The bridge here was stone and had fallen in the middle. The rushing waters danced with the falling sun and raced along the cut bank.

"Do you even have a plan for finding this crown? If it is here?" The Gypsy slid off and looked down the bank. "I honestly don't know where to start."

"This part of the river runs deep, into the caverns under the Mother." The Hunter pulled off his bow and quiver, setting them in a pile near the Stag's head. He rolled up his cloth pants and put his jacket and antler crown on the pile. "In my belongings is a book, with a blue cover. Pull it out for me?" he asked the Gypsy, who stared in a moment of confusion, but realization swept over her, and she dug into his rolled bundles.

"Siryns. I didn't think there were any still alive."

"No one knows for sure, but if anyone has something human that fell into the water, one of the Siryns probably does." He sat at the edge of the water and dipped his legs in one at a time.

The swirling waters calmed, and he pulled out a rope necklace he had hidden under his shirt. He twisted it until a flat, iridescent scale was at the front, and he gave a long, low whistle over the dark water.

The glossy surface was broken by gentle ripples, and two violet eyes peeked out over the water. Thick, deep-blue hair stuck to the dark skin as a face rose from the abyss, patches of blue scales shimmering on one side. Shells and bits of shiny rocks hung from her fin-like ears.

"What a pleasant surprise this is, a human that knows the Siryn's call." Her voice only added to her young feminine appearance, and her neck flared out as three sets of gills opened to the air. She glided through the water until she was almost touching the Hunter's legs.

"Would you be interested in a trade, words for a lost thing?" The Hunter wasn't fazed by the creature's closeness, though a small pang of jealousy reverberated through the Witch's gut as she handed him the blue book.

"How many words? What kind of lost thing?" Her hands came up, webbed fingers and arms covered in a blue, scaly skin made a half-hearted grab for the book before disappearing under the surface again.

"Long ago, before the fog took over the night, a boy fell into the water and dropped a ring of flowers."

"Not many are left from before the fog, did this boy make it out of the water?" Her eyes never left the book in the Hunter's lap as she spoke.

"It's assumed so."

"How many words?" she asked again.

"Three hundred pages, each covered in Dramba wax, so you can bring it under water." The Siryn licked her lips with a black, forked tongue as she stared hungrily at the book.

"I go and ask the elders about your flowers, too late tonight, the fog chokes us, and we die. At sunrise, you call again." She barely waited before turning and diving into the deep, her shimmering tail cresting the surface before her huge fin flashed in front of the Hunter, showering him with mist.

"Well, that went well." The Witch crossed her arms and looked at the Hunter.

"It was worth a try. I guess we'll sleep at the closest prayer camp on this trail and come back at daybreak. As soon as that sun sets, the fog will rush in, and I don't want to be stuck in it more than I have to."

Winter's Heir

Chapter Thirty-Two

Cedric reached out and touched the rough, brown bark where the Mother met the earth. Night had fallen in Da'nu, and the glowing flowers and leaves had all opened around the Temple of the Mother, a hand-laid, stone-block floor that circled the whole base of the tree. A bronze archway, tall enough for even a dragon to pass through, stood regally against the trunk, ancient words and symbols engraved into its surface.

Behind him, a small fire had been set up, and their three tents stood around it. The dwarves had slept through almost the entire trip up the hill and sat next to the fire, wrapped in a colorful woven blanket, sipping on Jar'ra's tea. Their eyes were yellow and bloodshot, and their skin was a sickly green, so dried and cracked that it had bled in places.

The two horses and Snow Bringer stood together in the colorful bushes and flowers, partially grazing but mostly falling asleep under the Mother's shadow.

"How long should we wait up for him?" Jar'ra called out to Cedric. After riding for a whole night and day to get here, her body felt ready to collapse onto the thick mat in her tent.

"Sephr?" Cedric walked over to the fire and kicked a stick farther into the flames with his boot. "Honestly, I was happy to be rid of his pessimism."

"I know, not many find him... friendly." Jar'ra sat in the entrance to her tent. "He's honestly a good person. He's just aggressive, especially around anything that could hurt his ego."

"I have a few other words I would have used, but I understand. In the army, there was a man we called the Wall. No one knew for sure why, but he had a huge scar from the bridge of his nose to the top of his head." Cedric sat at his tent next to her and pulled out his sack of dried fruit strips. "It looked like he had caught a sword with a faulty helmet right between his eyes but lived. He was like a boulder rolling down a hill; horses couldn't even stop him, but he couldn't talk and got aggravated easily."

"What happened to him?" Jar'ra wrapped her blanket around her knees and yawned deeply.

"He went head-on with a rhino in the Arena Games to try to raise his rank. It didn't end well."

"I've heard of the Arena. Brutal place."

"Brutal?" Cedric chuckled depressively. "Yeah, that's one word for it."

Jar'ra almost fell back with the force of a yawn, and she looked down the hill into the radiant jungle.

"I hope he's all right, but I'm too tired to stay up anymore."

"Get some sleep, Jar'ra. Now that I'm here, I don't know if I'll get any sleep. The dwarves need to go in tonight, so I will keep first watch?"

"All right. Good night, Cedric."

"Good night." He watched her crawl into her tent, and he turned to look at the two identical dwarves warming themselves by the fire.

"Almost ready?"

"Yes—"

"—I'm ready."

Winter's Heir

***

"It's been a long time since I've been to this side of the Mother." The Gypsy Witch leaned on the Hunter, her coal-black hair resting lightly on his shoulder. His arm wrapped around her and softly settled on her hip, holding her close. They looked out over the broken bridge and the dark forest to Spring Meadows that lay beyond. Quiet, rolling hills looked like frozen waves of clover, and the lights from the capital city poured over into the night sky, staining it with yellows and reds.

"It's a long time since you've been anywhere, Gust." He kissed her forehead. "Is your shoulder hurting?"

"Not as much as I thought it would, and the bleeding has stopped." She pushed her sleeve off her shoulder and the cloth wrappings were still clean.

"Good. Then maybe this little side trip won't do too much damage."

"This time tomorrow, we will meet up with everyone at the Mother, with the crown. And we have to accept that we were wrong."

"It's still hard to swallow that my twin brother not only had a romance for several thousand years but was going to ask her hand, and he never even told me about her."

"Maybe he was afraid you would be angry with him?"

"Angry that he had found a love? He should know better."

" He always came to the festivals and celebrations… That's what I don't understand." The Gypsy shifted until she was looking him in the eye. "He was always shy when it came to people, but he always showed up for the parades and festivals… He was fine and normal every time we saw him, until the Betrayal."

"Perhaps, it wasn't a betrayal at all." He looked off over the hill and pulled her closer. "Perhaps there is a better reason, and when we find the crown in the morning and bring it to the Mother, maybe we will find out what happened."

"Perhaps." The Gypsy yawned as she lay her head against his shoulder, closing her eyes and enjoying his earthy smell.

Chapter Thirty-Three

"Little Bird." The Hunter's rough fingers traced the edge of the Gypsy's cheek, who tenderly turned into the warmth of his hand.

"Little Bird? You haven't called me that since we were children."

"When was the last time you watched the sun chase away the night from the south side of the forest?"

"Around the same time you last called me 'Little Bird.'" She smiled. The Hunter's hand pulled away, and the Gypsy opened her hazel eyes just in time to see a flash of his dark, forest-green circles before his face rose out of view.

"Come, my love." He pulled her up and hugged her deeply. "We have a chance to clear my brother's name today, and I don't want to waste any time."

"I'm awake, I'm awake."

As the sun cut into the sky with an explosion of reds and pinks, the Hunter and the Gypsy watched the line of shadowy fog as it was pushed back from the river and into the thick, black forest beyond. The Stag carried them down the hill, his split hooves finding footing on the uneven ground. They dismounted when they got to the riverbank, and the Hunter stripped down to just his light pants, that he rolled up over his knees. He held the book in his lap as he dipped his legs into the cold water and sang the long, low whistle over the deep blue.

Rings rippled out from the calm as shells and bits of tumbled glass rose out of the abyss and lit up in the pure sunlight. A delicate crown of shells and pearls held together with long strings of water weed, sat on almost white braided hair. Mud-colored skin was half-covered with patches of glittery, white scales, and clouded, light-blue eyes looked out above the surface.

"Who is this man who knows the Siryn's Call?" Her voice was as strong and commanding as she was.

"I am the Guardian of the Forest of All, the Hunter."

"How did you get a scale of our people?" She swam closer, and two more heads rose from the water. Their violet eyes never left their elder, and dark-blue hair was braided back in small, tight rows.

The Hunter looked sheepishly at the Gypsy for a split second before looking back at the Siryn floating only a few feet in front of him in the river.

"Before the fog, I knew Key'ra. She gave it to me."

"Most are too young to remember a time before the fog, the Night Eater. I was still a child, playing in the water weeds when we could no longer see the moon, no longer count the stars." She pushed up against the hard dirt of the bank with her webbed hands, naked to the air except for the scales that spiraled over her skin. "I hear you are looking for a lost thing, Guardian of the Forest?"

"A simple ring of white flowers, a crown gifted from the Mother."

"And you have words to trade?"

"First of a series." He held out the book for her to look at, but she barely even glanced at it. One of the other Siryns swam forward and held a simple driftwood box out to the elder as she sat on the shore next to the Hunter, her long, shimmering tail started at her waist as a deep blue but faded into white by her fin as it floated to the surface.

"I accept it as a fair trade." She opened the driftwood box.

The blossoms still looked new, a perfect ring of flawless flowers, forever trapped just a moment before completely unfolding. It glowed and pulsed with the pure power of the Mother, reflecting off the elder's white and the two's blue scales. She held out the box for him to take and one of the watchers snatched the book out of his hands and dove, splashing water up with her dark-blue tail fin.

"It is true then," the Hunter whispered as he took the box, careful to not disturb the petals inside. "Thank you for keeping it safe."

***

Cedric didn't even know that he had fallen asleep until heavy footsteps on the old stone jarred him awake. He grabbed the frozen sword and rushed out of his tent, ready to take on anything that threatened their group, but after several moments of standing with the icy blade drawn, he realized the sound he heard echoed up from the tunnel behind the bronze archway. He sheathed the sword and waited as the sound grew louder.

The man that emerged from the depths of the Mother was huge, close to nine feet tall and built like a bear. He wore a simple white shirt that opened about halfway down the man's sculpted chest, and a jacket of dark-grey fur sat over his shoulder. Dark-brown hair was loosely braided and set with metal beads, even his beard had a short braid in the middle. The torch he held looked almost miniature in his huge hand.

"Cedric, she has been waiting for you." Cedric stepped back for a moment, but something about his voice made him think he knew this man, but it was too deep.

"Who are you?" His hand instinctively rested on the hilt of his sword. The man looked him over for a moment, then went down to one knee and looked Cedric in the eye with an uneven smile. When he looked deep into the waves of chocolate brown, Cedric knew.

"The dwarves?"

"I am Toma'rok, son of Baru'ma, of the mountains to the north, but call me Tom, the Explorer. The only successful one in the past twenty-five years!"

"But there were three of you?"

"They were all me, but that's a story for another time. The Mother has been expecting you, don't delay." Tom's pat on Cedric's shoulder almost made his legs buckle from the weight. "You look so much like your father, it's extraordinary."

"You knew my father?"

"Aye. A magnificent Guardian was he, of his land and his people. Respected by all. As you will be, once you come back to the Winterlands. Now go, it's not right to keep the Mother waiting." Tom stood and offered Cedric his torch, who gave the giant one last look as he turned to the bronze archway.

Chapter Thirty-Four

Soft yellow and orange danced around the gray-stone tunnel as Cedric took one stair at a time down into the depths of Da'nu. The air grew cold and damp, frosting his breath as he went farther and farther. The echo of his boots against the carved stone and his heart in his ears chanted around him like drums in the cavernous passageway. His mind raced with hundreds of questions he wanted to ask the Mother Tree, and he became so focused on the wording of each question that when his boot splashed on the next step, it made him jump in surprise.

The darkness fell away as a wave of light flowed through the cave. Small orbs of soft blue danced out from the center of the space, decorating the ceiling and banishing the shadows.

Three other staircases were cut out of the walls, each decorated with their own archway. The Winterlands stood to his left, the clear ice giving its own glow in the dim light. Across the water was the wood archway for Spring Meadows, and small, green buds speckled the carved words. The Summer Sanctuary sat to his right, its solid, bright gold demanding attention.

The orbs floated together at the top of the cave, piling over each other as more poured into the space. They hung down until they touched the surface of the water, and the column of soothing blue twisted and swirled in a solid cloud. The blue faded to white, and a woman stepped out of the whirlwind onto the surface of the water.

"Cedric Youngmoore." Her voice filled the space with melody and power as it bounced around the smooth walls. Her bare feet, hands, and face were pale but vibrant, made more of light itself than a real color. A simple white strip wrapped around her torso and down her legs, both covering and accenting her perfect form. "I have waited so long to meet you, my son." She cradled her hands over her chest. "My heart has broken for you."

Cedric felt his heart skip a beat and couldn't take his eyes off the vision in front of him. His thoughts went blank, lost in the glow of her power. She was so stunning and full of celestial power his mind couldn't completely process her.

"Mother," he whispered and took two trance-like steps down into the water.

"This was not how your life was supposed to be." She walked across the water, barely disturbing the fragile surface as tiny ripples flowed away from her. "I had so much planned for you, sweet child. You were going to be a warrior, a proud boy of proud blood."

"I am a warrior, Mother," Cedric spoke as the water rose over his knees.

"I know, my child. You have made so much out of so little, but you have so much left to do!" She knelt and cupped his cheeks with her hands. He could feel the pressure of her fingers, her raw power rubbing against his skin. White eyes looked into his soul as he lost himself in her presence. "Time is running out, and you are right where you need to be. Be sure in your steps, every inch is a journey through your destiny. I have a gift for you." Her hand fell from his face and picked up the golden chain around his neck. "Behold, the armor of the Winterlands."

A small glass snowflake formed on the necklace and ice grew out from the pendant, covering his shoulders, chest and legs. Intricate, swirling designs drew themselves across the thick plates as they formed but left his chest plate blank. It was the same ice that formed his sword, strong and nearly flawless as it wrapped around him.

"Use it well, Cedric, Guardian of the Winterlands." She pulled away from him and backed up over the water.

"Wait, Mother! I have so much to ask you!"

"You will find your answers, dear son. Trust in fate." Her words reverberated around the room as her light went out, and Cedric was left standing almost to his chest in water, his torch casting shadows across the stone.

Chapter Thirty-Five

"My King..." A scared man peeked around the black, stone door into the throne room where Korva normally sat at this time of day. The huge room looked empty, and he considered returning to the guards' station without telling his king the news. He slowly rounded the corner in the servants' hallway, mindlessly crumpling the roll of paper in his hand. He had a sinking feeling in his gut that he had picked the short straw this morning.

"King Korva?" His voice shook as he leaned into the king's bedroom, but the red velvet bed covers were undisturbed, still tucked in from the maid's rounds. He closed the door as carefully as he could, and only one other place came to mind as to where his king might be.

"If he's not there, I'll pay Jonjo to take it to him later. Dumb brood can't read, won't know what he's walking into," he whispered to himself, and he backtracked down the simple hall and out into the main foyer. He walked past the huge, gold braziers that sat between every gaping arch and through a golden double door at the center of the far wall. A dining table, with elegant gold place settings for over a hundred, sat patiently waiting for its guests while snarling furry faces looked down from the walls. He almost jogged around it and into the corner, where the wall pushed open and into another plain hallway. A left, then a right where it forked off, and a thick wooden door stood propped open to the outside. He stopped for a moment and sighed.

"I know where he is. Shit." He pulled open the paper roll to make sure he had the information right. He'd hate to tell the king bad news, only to find he had read it wrong but frowned when the words didn't change. He could barely control his hands as he tried to re-roll the paper and slid out the door into the castle gardens.

"My King, are you here?" The man stumbled as his eyes adjusted to the bright light.

"What is it?" The king and Sun Riser were past the black, stone walls of the garden, standing in the gold grass fields.

"A letter. You received a letter."

"Can't this wait? It's time to collect the taxes, and it's my favorite part of the harvest." Korva had one foot in the saddle at the base of Sun Riser's neck and was about to swing on. The man wanted to wait, wanted to run back to his bed and throw up the dread that had turned to rocks in his gut.

"I'm sorry, sir. I think you need to see this now. It's from Spring Meadows." Korva stopped.

"Spring Meadows?"

"Yes, Your Grace." Korva stepped down onto the grass and waited for the man to come to him.

"Hurry up now. I haven't got all day."

"Yes, My King!" He rushed over to him and put the crumpled roll into his king's hand. "May I leave, My King?" Korva didn't answer, but the man slipped away anyway, not willing to be there to take the brunt if he didn't have to be.

King Korva, of the Summer Sanctuary,

I am sorry it has taken me so long to write back to you. My time has been better spent preparing for the Spring Festivals. It must be terrible, being so lonely that you reach out to me for companionship. What we had is long gone, Korva. You clarified that when you cut down the Winter King and stuck your flag in half of Da'nu. Though I am sure you meant only the best by it, I don't understand how you think I would ever accept your hand in your current state. What you were when I loved you, and what you have become are incompatible. Please, if you do love me still, stay away from me and my lands. We would not survive in your shadow.

May the Mother guide you,

Petal Dancer, Guardian of Spring Meadows.

"No." Korva's rage flared in his red eyes as he ripped, crumpled, and threw the pieces of the letter. "NO! I will not be denied! 'May the Mother guide you'... Mother, where are you now!?" He stomped on the shreds of paper. "Where are you now, when your son is about to destroy your precious world?" The king grabbed onto Sun Riser's saddle and pulled himself onto the dragon's back. "We will burn it to the ground and raise our own in its place. Starting with that damned forest. UP, Dar E'um!" Sun Riser roared over the golden waves of prairie grasses as he ran, picking up speed before stretching open his vast leather wings and leaping into the air with his powerful hind legs. Hot air drifts from the summer sun lifted the huge beast, and with a tilt of the tip of one wing, they glided high above the land to the dark forest, the massive shadow of Sun Riser following them along the faraway ground.

Chapter Thirty-Six

The Stag's muscular legs fought to gain ground as he carried the Hunter and the Gypsy Witch up the hill, struggling to keep his pace. They were almost to the top, the dark-wood archway looming over them as the Mighty Stag huffed and puffed.

"You can do it, old boy. We're almost there," the Hunter urged the beast on until they burst onto the flat-stone platform. He quickly dismounted and helped the Gypsy down. "Quickly, get his saddle off. He needs to breathe and walk a moment." The Hunter slid leather out of the buckle and dropped the girth and giving the stirrup a pull, he caught the full weight of the saddle against his chest. "Gypsy, help!"

"Hunter." She stood stone still, looking off the hill over the division between Spring Meadows and the Summer Sanctuary. All the color had drained from her face, and she looked like she was about to cry. The Hunter dropped the saddle and supplies and tried to see over the glare of the sun.

A red blur appeared in the sky, so small he could barely see it against the horizon, but when the sun glinted off the streaks of gold that ran down the dragon's wings, his blood ran cold too.

"Sun Riser. What is he doing?"

"I don't know, but it can't be good. I highly doubt Korva wants to just talk."

"We need to hurry then and meet up with Cedric and the others before Korva gets here." They nodded, and grabbing only their weapons and the driftwood box, they went to the blooming archway.

"Well, won't you look at that, it does exist." Sephr walked out of the shadows in the tunnel, the hood of his cape pulled low over his eyes.

"Sephr, what are you doing here? Go tell Cedric—"

"No, Witch. I will not be that cowardly little fark's messenger boy," he spat his words like they were mixed with poison.

"Then let us pass so we can warn them! They'll never see him coming from the other side of the tree."

"I believe that is the idea." Sephr lifted his face. Glowing red eyes and a sickening smirk stared down the Gypsy. She gasped faintly.

"Sephr, what have you done?"

"Joined the winning side, like I always do." He pulled two knives from his belt and twirled them through his fingers. "I don't accept defeat. I don't accept failure. I will kill everything in this forest, and you will watch it burn to the ground!" He stopped the blades and pointed one at them. "I dare you to try to stop me. I don't lose."

"You have already lost, Sephr." The Witch's grip on her staff tightened down over the twisted bark, and the Hunter's fingers twitched in anticipation. A silent signal flew between them, and they both moved at the same time. The staff whistled through the air and caught Sephr in the throat as the Gypsy stepped forward. The Hunter took three steps back, held out his bow and let an arrow loose. As soon as the Gypsy pulled her staff away, the Hunter's arrow found its mark, and Sephr shrieked as his arm became painfully and bloodily pinned to the archway. He choked and gagged and gargled as he tried to pull his arm free, and another arrow dove into his lung. Sephr spat up blood as he tried to cough, and he shook as his weight gave out. Trapped to the archway, he couldn't do much more besides some half-hearted swipes with a contorted hand, before slumping into a pool of his own blood.

"Mother, I hope the others are all right." The Gypsy glanced over Sephr's body, as his white spirit slipped out of his nose and rose straight up into the branches of the Mother Tree. "He will find peace in her arms." She almost turned away when she thought she could see something dripping out of his mouth.

Dense, black liquid had dripped from the corner of Sephr's lip. As it rolled down his skin and over his clothes, it stuck to nothing and left no trail.

"What is that?" The Hunter leaned in to see as well, and when the liquid splashed onto the stone, it evaporated with a hiss. The fog pooled around his feet. "Oh no, Gypsy, it's the fog."

"I see that. It's going down the tunnel to the Mother. I can't stop it. I have no fire!"

"It will poison her. We need to do something!"

"Yelling at me won't make me think of it any faster!" The Gypsy felt over her many pouches and bags that hung on her waist, but no ideas came to her. She looked around frantically, but there was nothing useful, except the flint in their bags, but it would take too long to be able to use it. "I have an idea."

"What? What are you thinking?"

Winter's Heir

"Just take the crown and run ahead of me. Warn them about Sun Riser. Go!" The Gypsy gave the Hunter a shove down the tunnel.

Chapter Thirty-Seven

Cedric thought he could hear a sound echoing from behind him as he climbed the Autumn stairway to the light, but the tunnels were so large and the pool so vast, he supposed it must be an animal in one of the other regions scurrying in their tunnel. As soon as he could see the platform out of the archway, Jar'ra excitedly ran up to him and barraged him with questions.

"Wasn't that the single-most wonderful thing that has ever happened to you? I've read about it so many times. I can barely wait! Is she as beautiful as they say? Did she help you find your answers?" Cedric kept quiet with a compassionate smile as he let her run out of breath before trying to say anything.

"Why don't you go down there and find out? It's your turn, I believe." He laughed at her eagerness, not wanting to disappoint her with how little he had discovered. He was filled with something else now, a calm, sure feeling. He had a purpose, a drive to succeed in his goal, and he knew deep in his icy soul that he would have his answers along the way. Cedric handed the jumping Jar'ra the torch and watched as she tried to run down the tunnel steps.

"She's something else, isn't she?" Tom's deep voice carried from the campsite. "All fire and nowhere to put it."

"Jar'ra? She's been fun to travel with."

"She always is, like a walking library. Before Sephr got ahold of her, she was like that all the time."

"Did he…"

"Hit her? No, not like that. He's just… manipulative." Tom turned as Cedric walked to the fire, a pipe that must have been carved when he was a much smaller version of himself sat in his lips, hazy rings of violet smoke drifting away into the breeze. "I remember the day she appeared at camp. She had more chitter than all the birds like she never had anyone to talk to before. You could ask her anything, and she could quote at least two different scrolls and an artifact that told her the answer. And when she found out I was an explorer? That child never shut her—"

Cedric's eyes filled with white, and his body gave out, crumpling to the ground. He was abruptly out of breath, and his world spun as he tried to stop his lungs from screaming.

"Garuk." The word thundered against his soul and his heart missed a painful beat, but

when he opened his mouth to scream nothing came out. His eyes adjusted to the blinding colorless space, and he could see he was not alone. The Gypsy and the Hunter had fallen to one knee beside each other, touching shoulder to shoulder. Their eyes looked up at the center, shining bright hazel and emerald in turn. Jar'ra had crumpled to the ground, but she had pushed herself up almost to standing as she tried to shield her face from the light. Petal Dancer was in the same position as the Gypsy, her grey eyes like the beginnings of thunderclouds with light as her golden hair fell behind her and down the back of a dress that looked like a rose. The Mother floated in the center above them all, one hand pointing away from Cedric over the Gypsy's head. Sun Riser's deafening roar made Cedric clamp his hands over his ears and squeeze his eyes shut.

The ringing in his ears was so loud, Cedric didn't even hear Tom as he ran over and helped him to his feet. He opened his eyes to see the Hunter running out of the tunnel and moving his hands like he was shouting. The ringing dulled down as the Hunter pointed out over Cedric's shoulder, and a different kind of roar filled his ears.

"Fark."

The massive dragon glided over the outer rings of the Forest of All, molten fire misting from his mouth, igniting the dark, petrified forest in his path. The heat from the blazing forest helped to keep the beast lifted as his adept wings shifted and adjusted to ride the currents. The fire consumed the trees with an expanding roar.

"My camp, it's going to burn down the camp."

"He's going to light the whole damn forest."

"What do we do, Hunter?"

"How do you stop a fire-breathing dragon on a warpath?"

"You don't," Tom said, finding the humor in the Hunter's question.

"With water?"

"So, we wait for Petal Dancer to fight off the dragon with her thunderstorm and just pray he doesn't light the Mother before she gets here. That's a truly solid plan there, Cedric."

"Damn it, Tom, at least I'm trying."

"You could ask him to stop." Jar'ra's voice sounded small compared to the three burly men, but they all turned as soon as she made a sound.

"What?" Tom almost laughed but caught himself as he noticed how serious she was. "What makes you think that beast will listen to you?"

"The Mother told me he would. Please, Hunter, may I see your Kra?"

"Only Guardians can use the Kra, Jar'ra." But the Hunter took off the rope necklace and handed it to her, beside his protest. She twisted it around until she found a fleck of gold, like a broken piece of a much larger plate. She held it tightly in her fist and raised it into the air.

"Dar E'um! Garuk!"

Chapter Thirty-Eight

The Gypsy almost stumbled into the water under the Mother Tree in the near darkness. Feeling the hard steps with her feet, she waded further and further into the pool until she was in the center and up to her neck. She lifted her staff high and slammed it down as hard as she could, completely submerging it, and wedged the thin end into a notch she knew was there. Amber light poured from the head and covered the water, giving an almost orange glow to the rest of the room. She could see now that she had beaten the fog to the water as she sighed in relief, but only by about three steps. At first, the fog hissed and pulled back from the sudden light, but as more came crawling down the stairs, it swirled into itself, condensing and growing. An arm formed out of the mass, then another, then the legs and head, and a torso as it stood. It looked and flowed like a liquid. Thick, black drops fell from its fingertips and were absorbed by its feet.

"You dare try to stop me, Gypsy Witch?" The voice was almost as slick and slithery as its body was, and the way it seemed to get stuck on S's made the Gypsy's skin crawl. Without her staff, she was defenseless, but it needed to stay right where it was to protect the Mother.

"Every hour of every day!" she yelled.

"Then I'll just have to take care of you, won't I?" Its sick laugh bounced around the room, and it took a step onto the light. A thick ooze leaked from the darkness' feet and spread out just over the surface. It wasn't strong enough to get through the light into the water, but the figure melted as it enclosed the Mother's pool.

The Gypsy dove under the surface just before the slick blackness got to her, but when she tried to surface again, she found the flowing liquid had solidified. There wasn't even an inch of air she could use. She hit and pushed on the black shell, but it held firm, and her lungs were starting to burn.

Mother, I don't think I'm going to make it out of this one. She tried to put her lips to the surface to pull on the little bit of air there was, but only succeeded in sucking water into her lungs. She sputtered and choked, which brought in more water. Her head pounded as her throat tightened to try to stop the drowning, but the liquid was already doing its damage. Her mind flew through the milestones of her life. The day the great owl had chosen her to be his Guardian. The look on the Hunter's face when they had shared their first kiss. The feeling she had every time she looked into his emerald eyes.

She gave one last punch against the black surface before her body shut down and refused to move. The last thing she could see was the white wisp of her soul as her vision faded to black. Her fear and panic faded into calm, and a familiar voice surrounded her.

"You are in my arms now, child. No more harm will come to you."

***

"What are you doing, you dumb fark?!" Korva yelled against the wind from Sun Riser's saddle as he tugged against the reins to get the dragon to go back on course. Sun Riser ignored him completely, tilting until he was headed straight for the base of the Mother Tree. "We're going to crash, you idiot!"

Cedric was probably the most surprised out of the three men when the dragon stopped burning down the forest and made a sharp turn to face them.

"Holy Mother, he stopped." The Hunter was the only one looking at Jar'ra, and he could have sworn for a second that he could see flecks of gold in her eyes. As Sun Riser approached, he threw back his wings to brake himself, landing on his back legs as lightly as a feather, but when his front came crashing down, the whole ground shook, and everyone fell except Jar'ra. He roared and growled and put his massive, scaly snout inches from her face as if he tried to scare her, smoke billowing up into her eyes. She stood her ground, even when he turned to look at her with one red eye, and she realized it was bigger than her head. Her hand holding the Kra lowered, and she very slowly reached out to the animal.

"Hello, Sun Riser. Don't be afraid, no one is going to hurt you anymore."

"What are you whispering to my dragon, peasant?!" A very frustrated and angry Korva yelled from the base of Sun Riser's neck. He swung his leg over the saddle and climbed down.

Jar'ra hand grazed the center scale of Sun Riser's head, and it felt like the world exploded as a wave of energy burst from their cores.

"Stars of our ancestors," Tom muttered under his breath as he watched from the ground, "the birth of a Guardian."

Chapter Thirty-Nine

Coo'ara shot up as the sun touched the center of the sky, sweat cascading from her black hair and down her neck. She had taken to sleeping in the giant owl's nest in the Guardian's Grove when the Gypsy had started teaching her almost as soon as she could walk, and Wind Runner would sleep with her on occasion.

She had fallen asleep with the Gypsy's book over her violet eyes, the same one that now lay open on her lap maybe five pages from the end. Wind Runner's bulky wing lay over her and off the side of the oversized nest like a tent, but he too awoke with a start, and a loud quirky "Hoo!"

"I know," the small girl said, and she stretched out to pet the owl's face reassuringly.

His feathers felt soft against her little hand, and she got a sinking feeling in her gut when he didn't look at her that something wasn't right.

"It's not the Witch, is it, boy?" she asked the owl, who answered with a much quieter "Who" before jumping up out of the open ceiling to see out of the branches. Coo'ara climbed out of the downy nest and ran over to the open window, and what she saw nearly knocked the wind out of her.

Fire, consuming, raging fire roared all around the Guardian Grove and threatened to overtake it. The Hunter's Camp in the distance was in the same predicament, with a wall of fire quickly spreading through the dead forest into the new growth.

Wind Runner hopped back down into the room, tilting and twitching his head until he found what he was looking for hanging from pegs in the wall. He pecked at a simple strip of leather with handles, and Coo'ara thought it looked a little like a saddle, but without all the padding and fluff. She cautiously pulled it off the wall, and the massive owl bowed in front of her, so she could slip it over his head. Once it was positioned over his wings, the straps that remained across the front attached with a simple loop buckle to the other side.

"You ready, boy?" Coo'ara said shakily as she finished tightening everything. Wind Runner turned his body but kept his head looking at the girl as she slipped her hands and feet into the straps. He hopped around to adjust to the added weight before jumping up over the wall into the intertwining branches and spreading his wings. She could just barely see over the gigantic owl's shoulder, and from her view, it looked like the whole world was burning. Fear threatened to strangle her gut as the smoke stung her eyes and throat.

Wind Runner dropped out of the tree and beat hard to gain access into the air. He soared around and up out of the branches, continuing a fluid spiral until they were safely above the flames. The bird flew like he had a mission, knowing exactly where to take the girl to safety as he turned to go into Autumn Fall.

Coo'ara sighed in relief at seeing the burning forest fall away from her, but she still twisted her hands around the straps to make sure she would not fall off. They leveled out and just glided for a time. She had never ridden the owl before, but she had sat through enough stories to know it was possible. The wind kicked up, tossing the girl's thick, black hair over her back and ruffling Wind Runner's feathers. One feather fluttered over itself and landed on top of Coo'ara's hand.

Pure, hard power coursed into her and exploded out into the sky in an amber light, and it was like she could see for the first time after a life of being blind.

The world around her lit up in faintly colored threads, like a web of color that crisscrossed not only through Autumn Fall but connected all of Da'nu.

"The strings of fate. I see it now."

***

Korva had flown from his saddle in the explosion of power, bashing his head hard against the Mother Tree's tough bark before falling onto the stones of the platform. The king lay at the base of the tree, shattered and broken from his fall. He stared up at the sunlight filtering through the leaves, wondering if that was the last thing he would see. He could almost feel the soft, restful pull of everlasting sleep, a promise of freedom from his cage. Tears welled up in his emerald eyes, and he was thankful that at least his body was so broken, the darkness would have no use for it.

Do I hear you giving up, you weak, pathetic child?

Korva's hands erupted in pain as joints and bones twisted and snapped together under his skin. The scream of agony that ricocheted from his soul drowned in his punctured lungs, and by the time it made its way out, it was only a bloody gurgle.

We're so close. Can't you taste it?

His arms were jerked out and straightened, muscles reknit and soldered to newly reformed bone. The pain was excruciating, rocking through his body and sending him farther and farther into the darkness.

Winter's Heir

*I own you, Korva. Body, blood, and soul.
You think I would let you free so easily?*

Chapter Forty

Cedric felt like the blast of fiery light and energy had wiped his mind. He could barely remember who he was as he stared at Jar'ra, her brown eyes fading into a rich honey. Her hand tenderly traced the veins of glittering gold through the deep red and orange scales on an immense, thorny head. Even her plain, brown hair had turned red at the roots. He felt frozen as his mind tried to reassemble itself and process what he was seeing.

"Korva. Where's Korva?" The Hunter pushed himself up and went to help Tom.

"I can't believe that worked." Jar'ra sighed and laughed as the adrenaline of the moment faded. "Did anyone see that?"

"We all saw it, Jar'ra, but how?" Cedric stood and dusted off his pants. "Did you... bond with Sun Riser?"

"Has anyone seen Korva? We're still in danger." The Hunter's gruff voice failed to grab everyone's attention, but the flash of color and heavy thud behind them at the base of the Mother Tree certainly did.

"Found him." Tom pointed and chuckled lightly, but the Hunter pinched the bridge of his nose and shook his head.

"Yes... yes, you did." The Hunter walked over to examine his brother.

"Well, if I didn't know any better, I'd say he was dead." The impact against the tree had shattered the man's body, his limbs lay in a tangled mess around him. The Hunter looked at Korva's face, emerald eyes glazed over as they stared into the branches, brown, curly hair unkempt for so long it matted, and he whispered softly as he opened the driftwood box.

"Brother, why did you never call for me? If you needed help, all that was required was for you to ask me, and I would have rushed to your side." As the lid fell open and the brilliant, white light of the blossom crown fell onto Korva. The Hunter watched as an unseen force seemed to grab the man's contorted hands and feet, pulling them away from the core of his body. Fingers realigned with nauseating snaps.

"Hunter, what's happening?" Tom offered his assistance, but the Hunter held up his hand to stop him.

"The darkness is healing his body." He took the crown and laid the box on the stone but sat and watched as Korva's beaten body reformed. "If I wait to cast out the evil until his body is healed, he might have a chance to survive. After thirty years, I want to give him the best chance I can."

"You really want to save him? After all he's done? Threw all Da'nu into chaos, murdered guardians... I'd let him die."

"It wasn't him, Tom. I know that now. Korva was never capable of this kind of violence, he was the creating one. I was the killer." He pushed back a brown curl from his brother's face as Korva's chest twisted and snapped. He heaved in air as his ribs freed his lungs and spasmed as blood tried to find a way out.

"Almost..." The Hunter held the glowing blossom crown over his brother's head as the man was finally able to scream. Korva's back arched as the pieces of his spine slid and clicked into place. The Hunter could only imagine the kind of pain his brother was going through, but he knew what had to be done.

"Now." The crown slid onto Korva's head as the last few bones and muscle found their place, and the Hunter held it on. He watched as the flowers absorbed the darkness out of his brother, fading out of their pure white into shades of gray, as Korva's body seized. Hands grabbed and ripped at the Hunter's clothes, but Tom held Korva down as the man's screams hollowed and darkened. The Darkness burned through his core, and the petals of the blossom crown withered and bunched up.

"You cannot destroy me! I am everything!" A slick, lispy voice shot out of Korva's mouth, poisonous and powerful in its words. The Darkness sunk its claws as deep into Korva's soul as it could, unwilling to release its prize. "No mortal can destroy the immortal!"

"Free my brother! You are nothing more than a creation, like the birds or the Siryns. All creations can be destroyed by the power of the Mother." The Hunter watched as the crown grew darker, the outer petals turning to ash and falling away. Korva's eyes flared into deep, fiery reds and oranges, burning out the blackness as it was finally torn from him, before fading out into their dazzling emerald. His body relaxed, sinking into Tom and his brother's arms. The battle, the one he had fought for thirty years to not forget himself, had ended with almost the same suddenness it had begun. The darkness was gone from Korva, but the Hunter could feel the war was not over.

"Korva? Korva, can you hear me?" The Hunter shook him, but his brother's body stayed limp in his hands. "We have to bring him into the Temple. Help me, Tom." He took the dying crown carefully off his brother's head, and the giant man draped Korva over his shoulder. "Cedric, Jar'ra, stay here. We'll be back."

Winter's Heir

Chapter Forty-One

The shadow of Wind Runner floated over the orchards and villages of Autumn Fall, the giant owl knew exactly where they were going. Far in the highlands, near the edge of the perfect harvest hills, lay a small collection of grass huts, with one standing in the middle, decorated with colorful fabrics and amber ties. The Village of the Guardian, Wind Runner's Rest, Gypsy's Place, this patch of land was known by many names, but due to its location high in the Autumn Hills, it was hard to get to on foot, so most men outside of those who lived there had never seen it. Those who had chosen to live beside the Guardian were well protected but survived on the offerings that the rest of the land brought to them.

Wind Runner circled over the village, and Coo'ara could see the ant-sized humans come out from their homes to greet them. Their clothes were simple and hand woven, looking more like a dress with a vine belt. Some had feathers and stones woven into their hair, others wore theirs in braids with amber holdings. Coo'ara had read of this place from the Gypsy's book, but it still had her in awe as the owl came to a graceful landing.

Her muscles ached from gripping the saddle, and she almost fell off as they touched down, but strong bronze arms caught her before she hit the ground.

"What is happening? It looks like the whole forest is on fire!" Coo'ara could barely see in the mass of color as the villagers surrounded her, not just from their strings, but their dress. Feathers, beads, and dark hair swung in front of her face, and hands pulled her up to standing. She felt weak and tired, words would not form even though she tried to speak.

"Give her space. We can't imagine what she's going through." A sweet, soft voice rang out over the faces and their movement stopped. Coo'ara's vision went white, and the woman's voice rang out in her blindness. "Hush now, child, you are safe."

***

The Hunter took deliberate, careful steps down into the dark depths of the Temple of the Mother, Tom only a few steps behind him with Korva on his back. He slowly passed his torch so its light went from one wall to the other, sure that something was wrong but unable to find any sign of it as they made their descent.

"Gypsy, Gypsy, can you hear me?" His voice echoed back to him in the darkness, and he could feel its empty response in his soul like a dagger to the gut. They stepped down into the cavern, and a deep, throaty laugh encircled them.

"What an honor. The Brave Hunter of the Forest of All, coming to the aid of his beautiful Gypsy Sweetheart, and I am alive to see it. I, Darkness and all that is, cannot be destroyed!"

A brilliant flash of white light exploded from the center of the space, filling it and casting down the darkness. The Mother appeared, standing in all her pure-white form above the surface. Her bare feet did not touch the darkness, though a hiss erupted from it like a cornered animal.

"You have nowhere to run now, light above and light below. Die an honorable death, do not fight it," the Mother's sweet, gentle voice filled the void that the darkness had made as it bubbled and boiled from the light. It hissed and screamed, rippled and boiled. The sounds were stomach wrenching and gut turning, even the Hunter held his hands over his ears against the assault.

The ground beneath their feet shook, and the stone walls showered them with dust.

"Take cover!" The Hunter yelled back to Tom before falling down and covering his head. The light became so intense, it burned his eyes through his lids.

Chapter Forty-Two

Every citizen of Da'nu stood still in fear as the dirt beneath their feet shook. Children clung to their parents' legs, eyes closed tight against the chaos around them. The brilliant, blinding, pure-white light flew out from the Mother Tree and raced across the land, bathing everything from the smallest insect to the tallest tree. The haunting chorus of thousands of twisted monsters filled the air and could be heard all the way in the Winterland mountains as darkness was ripped from their bodies. Da'nu shifted in that moment, reverting its former self. The dirt healed, the air cleared, and the waters became calm once more.

The birds were the first to celebrate, their chitter growing to a deafening roar as the dust settled. Howls, roars, and barks followed, then the people finally realized what had happened, and they joined in with their own cheers and hurrahs.

To Cedric and Jar'ra, standing at the foot of the Mother overlooking Da'nu, it sounded like the whole world was singing. They watched as the beautiful light transformed the land, inch by inch, foot by foot. It was a stunning display of the Mother's healing power, and they couldn't help but join in the happiness, embracing each other almost suddenly. They didn't even notice the quiet wing beats and soft hooves that landed behind them as Petal Dancer and her winged Companion came to a stop by their camp.

The thin, blonde woman dismounted and if Snow Bringer hadn't whinnied at their arrival, Cedric and Jar'ra may have never noticed they were even there.

"What a wonderful day this turned out to be," Petal Dancer almost sang as she approached the two who now stood side by side. "Not only did you save Da'nu and the Mother Tree, but it looks like Summer has finally found its rightful Guardian." She smiled brightly at Jar'ra and touched her cheek with her fingertips. "You look so much like your mother."

Cedric couldn't take his eyes off Petal Dancer. The way her hair fell over her shoulders and flowed like water whenever she moved held him in a trance. She was more stunning up close than she was from a distance, and his mind wandered into the land of 'what if.'

"Where is the Hunter?" Petal asked as she admired how calm Sun Riser seemed.

"He went under the Mother with Tom and Korva. I think the Gypsy is down there too."

Winter's Heir

***

The Hunter slowly waded into the water, now clear of the darkness, to where the Mother knelt on the surface.

"No..." he whispered softly, and his voice shook like a child. "No, Little Bird, it's not supposed to be like this." He didn't even care that his coat and pants would be soaked as he watched the Gypsy's body as it floated in the water. Her eyes were closed, as if she had fallen asleep beneath the surface, but it was a sleep he knew she would never wake from.

"She gave her life to save me, Hunter, to save all of us." The Mother's slow, melodic words did nothing to comfort him as his hand reached his love, feeling how cold she had become.

"She can't truly be gone."

"Her spirit has left its shell." He pulled her body close to his, studying her features like it was the first time he saw her. The way her thick, black hair floated around her like a halo, the perfectly imperfect way her lips met each other, the smallness of her fingers against his rough ones.

"Can nothing be done?" He tried his best but failed to hide the desperation in his voice.

"Not for her body, no." The Mother stood and raised her arms. "I can make no promises, Hunter. Her soul has already accepted its death, but I will see what can be done."

Behind them, Tom had lowered Korva's thrashed body off his shoulder so that it floated in the Mother's healing waters. He watched as it glowed where it touched Korva's skin, and the man's eyes slowly opened. They had been restored to their vibrant green but were covered in a cloud-like haze as they stayed fixed straight ahead.

It was a long, tense moment before Korva sat straight up in the water, coughing and sputtering and patting himself down. He had looked death straight in the eye, and yet, he had air in his lungs, and his heart beat heavily in his chest. He couldn't believe he had survived somehow through all these years, trapped just underneath his own consciousness.

"Welcome back." Tom crossed his arms and shook his head. He didn't trust Korva even for a second.

"I'm... I'm here." He almost laughed roughly in relief, touching his own face and pulling on his wet clothes. "I'm not dead!"

"You would have been if it were up to me."

"How... how long was I out?"

"After you hit the tree? A few minutes."

"No, I mean... how long has it been since the darkness took over?"

"You really don't know?" Tom relaxed his shoulders a bit and sighed. "Korva, it's been twenty-five years since you first tried to attack the Mother."

"Attack? No, never. I would never..." but he stopped. "Oh Mother, what have I done." Tears welled up in his eyes as it all flooded in. "Oh Mother, I killed them, didn't I? I'm a murderer... A farking murderer." He tried to close his eyes against the torrent of memories that threatened to overwhelm him, against the pain that tightened around his chest. "What have I done... I mixed up everything."

The Mother walked over to him, kneeling to put her hands on the sides of his face.

"You have a lot to atone for, my son, but it wasn't entirely your fault."

"How could I do all these horrible things? I'm a monster," he said through tears with a shaky voice.

"No, the darkness was the monster. You only let it consume you in your fear. I blame myself for not being able to save you from it." The Hunter took notice of nothing other than the Witch, unmoving in his arms. He didn't know what to say to his brother. He had no more words in him. He didn't even have the energy to be angry, or forgiving, or anything else.

"Tom. Can you help me get her out of the water?" he finally croaked out.

Chapter Forty-Three

The fire was crowded as night took over again, but there was a peace in the air that wasn't there before. Sun Riser had curled in a ball against the trunk and roots of the Mother with Jar'ra asleep under his wing. Snow Bringer and Rain Dancer ran and played together, like they were young foals again. The glistening pastel trail left by the perly horn followed by Snow Bringer's flurries in a revolving circle. Only the Hunter and his Stag were missing from the group, having rode off to find calm in the forest. Cedric had done his best to freeze the Gypsy Witch so that time would have no effect on her body. Petal had said that the Guardian needed to be returned to her people, so they could morn her properly.

Cedric could feel the questions stick in his throat as he watched Petal and Korva discuss all that had happened, unwilling to interrupt their reconnection but feeling the jealousy in him like a hot coal in his stomach. Sooner or later, he would have to cough it out.

This was the woman he had sketched when he couldn't sleep, dreamed about when he could, and he couldn't swallow the idea that Korva was her rightful lover, not him.

"It's just not right," he muttered quietly under his breath. When Petal's gentle smile leaned in and kissed Korva on the forehead, he finally had enough. He couldn't sit there and just take it anymore. "I need to think," he grumbled and left the campsite, taking the winding path down the hill and didn't care if anyone would want to follow.

He hated himself for feeling like this. He could kill a thousand men without feeling a thing, but when it came to that woman, it was like he lost all common sense and acted like a child. He had no right to assume he could just ride in and claim her like she was a nice table or a family inheritance. She was a woman, and a woman who barely knew him at that. "Why does Korva get a second chance before I even get a first one?" he said to the wind as he kicked a pebble in his path. It rolled down the hill and came to a soft, sudden thunk as it hit another stone and stopped.

"Winter Guardian! I was just coming up to see the Mother!" It was the Drum'ma, and the stone that Cedric's pebble had hit was actually a paw.

"Oh, hello. Sorry about that. I'm not myself right now." He tried to collect his thoughts, so he didn't make a fool of himself in front of the stone being.

"I can smell it, sickly sweet, a poison in your heart. What happened up there?" It seemed genuinely inquisitive as it leaned down to look him in the eye with its quartz ones. Cedric didn't answer, just looked down at his boots to avoid the Drum'ma's gaze. "Hmm... best not to let these things fester within you. Poison will not cure itself, you know."

"I know. I just need to walk for a moment, collect myself."

"As you wish but mark my words, Guardian. Darkness begins in the heart."

***

With a heart as heavy as stone, the Hunter and his Stag slowly plodded through the jungle-like underbrush of the forest. His thoughts were on the past, trying to remember every detail of his beloved Witch. He could almost picture her, running through her orchards, dancing with her wind as a child. As she grew into a woman, her grace and wonder only increasing to him as the ages flew by. He vowed he would never forget the way she moved, swaying and twisting with each little gust. The sound of her voice as she would say his name.

"Hunter." As sweet as honey dripping off the comb, he could almost hear her saying it. "Hunter, turn around."

The Stag stopped in his tracks, and the Hunter realized he wasn't hearing her voice out of grief. He turned in the saddle, and the vision standing there knocked the air from his lungs.

Pure white from the tips of her bare feet to her hair high on her head, his love stood in the forest as solid as the trees around them. Her dandelion crown had been replaced with a small ring of antlers, a miniature to his own. A simple, white slip covered her form almost to her knees.

At her feet, a small, white fawn lay in a ball. The Hunter blinked and rubbed his face in disbelief.

"You... you're here."

"I am." Her gentle smile was almost too much for him. He dismounted and slowly walked to her, reaching out a hand to touch her to make sure she wasn't a dream. Rough shaking fingers met her warm shoulder, and he scooped her up into his arms. The tears finally flooded out as he buried his face into her breasts.

"You're alive. Oh Mother, you're alive!" She softly ran her fingers through the hair on the back of his neck as he held her tight, afraid that if he let her go, she would disappear into the wind.

"The Mother has remade me. I am to remain here, in the forest. We can be together now." The Hunter wept. Grateful, pain-filled tears stained her clothes.

"I thought… I was so lost… I couldn't see the world without you in it." He lifted his head to stare into her now-gray eyes, and she wiped away his tears with her thumbs before kissing him deeply. Her legs wrapped around his hips, and they stayed in that moment, completely entwined into each other, each unwilling to bring it to an end. "I thought I had lost you forever."

"Never my love. I will be with you always."

Chapter Forty-Four

Sun Riser nuzzled the sleeping form of Jar'ra closer to his belly from under his wing, blowing his hot breath over her when he felt her shiver. The change was happening much faster than it ever had before, her hair almost completely blood red in the few hours since they had joined. He knew he had made the right choice. He could smell the Summer in her like she was made of sunshine and fire, and he finally felt complete and sure of his actions for the first time since Ember had died so many years ago. Closing his golden eyes, he reached out to her on the link they shared, knowing it was time to show her the dreams. It was on him to show her the past, her past.

Winter's Heir

Jar'ra felt like she was flying, the wind roughly whipping her hair against her face and stinging her eyes. She could see Sun Riser beside her, his golden streaks shining and glittering along his body and down his tail as his massive wings fought hard against his weight to stay airborne. A woman sat at the base of his shoulders, her own fiery hair braided tightly in a single, long row that whipped behind her. Thin, golden armor plates ran along her arms, legs, and spine, interlocking and nearly seamless. She had no saddle, no reins, but it didn't seem to bother her as Sun Riser leaned hard into a turn, leveling back out with the Mother Tree ahead of them on the horizon.

"For the Mother!" she shouted, pumping her fist into the air.

A scream of pain, so high pitched and terrifying that Jar'ra couldn't help but close her eyes and shy away from it, and she found herself on her hands and knees on a black, stone floor.

"Please, my queen, you've almost done it." Women walked around Jar'ra and to a bed in the dark room. A tiny fire crackled in the only hearth, neglected in the chaos. The women were dressed in white, but there was so much blood splattered on everything, it made Jar'ra feel sick. Ember lay on the bed, a single, red sheet covering her breasts and twisted around her. A huge wound on her swollen belly had opened as three women tried to hold fabric over it to stop the bleeding, yelling to the others for more towels and water.

"I need to push. I can't stop it!" Ember howled as her voice cracked, her desperation so strong that tears welled up in her eyes.

"Please, miss, we need to stop the bleeding..." but their voices were lost in another scream that was almost inhuman as Ember

gripped onto the sheet and a river of red came from between her legs.

Sharp harsh light poured into the room as a door was opened, and the Gypsy Witch ran in to Ember's side.

"I'm here. I'm here now, Ember." The Witch grabbed her hand and stroked the strands of sweat-soaked hair off the woman's forehead.

"My husband... where is my husband?" she said between ragged breaths.

"I don't know, dear. I'm sure he's on his way..."

"I see a head!" one of the handmaidens yelled and four more came out of the shadows, all with fresh, white towels. "Oh Mother, there's so much blood..." Ember arched, and a deep, guttural noise racked her body, full of agony and frustration. More blood flowed, covering the

women in a sea of red up to their chests and a small, scared cry brought the room to silence.

"A son, Ember! You have a son!" It was like she couldn't hear the Witch, looking wildly around the room.

"Frost... Frost, where are you?" she whimpered.

"Keep pressure on the wound, girls! We need to stop the bleeding." The women rushed again, trying and failing to stop the flow.

"Gust?" It was no more than a squeak.

"Yes, I'm here." The Witch squeezed her hand and tried to look into her golden eyes. Ember's lips moved for a moment as they tried to form words, but as fear washed the color out of her face, she lost what she was going to say.

"Oh Mother on high... there's another head."

She was too exhausted to make more than a faint cracking as her eyes rolled into the back of her head, her body arching involuntary. There was a tense moment of near silence before the tiny, helpless cry echoed off the black-stone walls.

"A girl."

"Mother... Mother, take me home." The white wisp of her soul floating out of her mouth as the words went unnoticed by all but the Witch.

***

Reflections of the dying fire danced against the gray background of Petal Dancer's eyes as she contemplated the events that had unfolded before her. Yesterday, she would have tried to kill Korva, Killer of Guardians, but tonight, all she wanted was to hold him close and forget th¹e evil that had consumed him.

"We were all so wrong."

"Hmm?" Korva shook himself awake and looked over at the beautiful woman besid[2]e him.

"I had no idea... about the darkness... about everything. It killed me to write that letter, but you weren't you..."

"I know, my love. I can never take back the things I did. I can never fix them. But please know that I never stopped thinking about you, not for a single moment." The back of his hand gently stroked her cheek, and she leaned into it, closing her eyes. "You kept me alive in there, the mere thought I could see you again carried me in the darkness."

"Oh, why don't you just get married then?" Tom, who until then, had been dozing off across the fire, puffing lightly in his pipe. "It's damn

---

1
2

obvious. You've been in love since when? The beginning of time? Just go do the thing." Korva's hand stopped mid-stoke, and Petal's mouth suddenly hung open.

"What? No. I mean... the people. They wouldn't understand."

"Oh for fark's sake, can't you think about yourself for once, Petal? You're known throughout Da'nu because of the love the people have for you. You don't think they can trust you on this?" Tom tapped out his pipe on the stone before refilling it again. "The Mother already gave you her blessing. Just ride in there and get it done. I hear the castle gardens are lovely this time of year. Plus, I'm just about sick of you two acting like lovestruck youngins." Perfect rings of violet smoke popped from his pipe one after another in a long string as they rose into the branches.

"We couldn't possibly..."

"But why not? Petal, I've waited for centuries to be able to ask your hand... Since we were children, and I made flutterbugs for you to chase, and I watched your face open like a blooming rose. I knew that one day, I would stand before you and swear my eternity to you. I knew the first time we kissed, on the hill under the stars, that you were the only one I would ever love. I was never so sure of anything in all my years as the day I came to the Mother and asked for her blessing to marry you." He took her hand into his and shifted onto his knees. "Please, Colla, Guardian of Spring Meadows, grant me this one wish and let me stand at your side until the Mother takes back my soul."

Her pale skin flushed with pink, and placing her free hand over his, she said through teary eyes, "I grant you my hand, and for as long as I breathe, you shall stand with me, and I with you."

Winter's Heir

Chapter Forty-Five

By the time Cedric had finally decided to head back up the hill to camp, a new sun had begun to rise over Da'nu, and every animal buzzed with excitement over the news. He had thought that he could clear his head to the sound of the crashing waterfall by the bridge, but between the near-constant hooting of owls and the bright-neon trails of powder the fairies left through the air in the darkness, it was just too hard to reason past his emotions.

"What the fark is wrong with me? I can't think..." he said as if expecting himself to answer. Every time he tried to direct his thoughts somewhere else, they always came back to her. To Korva. To the thought of Korva and Petal dancing off into the sunset together, leaving him alone with gnawing jealousy ripping apart his gut. "She barely knows me, but I can change that. I have to show her I am worthy of her hand." He steeled himself as he rounded the last corner on the trail, but his heart sank even further when he reached the top.

Everyone was gone. Everyone except Tom and the Drum'ma who were deep in conversation, Snow Bringer, and the white horse.

"I can ensure safe passage out of the forest. Though the evil appears to have left our lands, there's still plenty of predator types who wouldn't mind making a meal of a horse slowed down by a cart."

"That would be helpful. We have a long ride ahead of us. Petal Dancer said she would send a cart to carry the Witch, and I plan to see to it that it makes it to her people."

"That's very noble of you."

"I don't consider it as noble, simply the right thing to do."

"Where is everyone?" Cedric finally spoke up and walked over to them.

"Ah Cedric, so good of you to join us! Have you cleared your head?"

"As much as I can, I suppose."

"Good, good. You have a long walk ahead of you, and you need to be clear of mind." It wasn't lost on him that Tom had avoided the question.

"Where is Petal?" He had to work not to grind his teeth.

"Well… she went back to Spring Meadows… with Korva." Cedric looked away, and the Drum'ma became interested in his reaction, tilting his stone head and leaning in slightly. He bit down hard on his tongue, forcing words back down his throat, and only stopped when he tasted blood. He didn't even have a chance to tell her goodbye.

"And Jar'ra?"

"She awoke in a panic about an hour ago, muttering something about bloodlines and parents, and she took off on Sun Riser. If I could have stopped her, I would have, but have you ever stood in front of a dragon and tried to tell it no?"

"No, I can't say I have."

"And pray you never will. Now come on, you have to pack your tent and get going."

"Where is it you think I'm going?" Cedric had been ready to throw the towel in on this whole adventure and slink back to the army, before he realized with Korva healed, there probably wouldn't be an army to slink back to.

"You have to go to the Winterlands... You are the Guardian, after all."

Winter's Heir

***

Coo'ara was thankful for the dimness of the light when her eyes finally opened. The small room was thick with the smell of burning herbs, and after a momentary panic at the smoke that rose to the low ceiling, she swung her legs over the edge of the cot and tried to look around. There was a small sliver of light cutting through the room as it escaped past the woven mat that hung over the doorway. An altar sat across from her, covered in gourds, carved figures, candles that had obviously been burning for hours, and a metal bowl which was the source of the herbal smoke. When her feet hit the floor, they were met with soft furs, and no sooner did she try to stand, the light suddenly became so blinding, she had to cover her eyes. A woman's voice filled the space.

"Welcome back to the living, child. Do you know where you are?"

"I... I think Wind Runner's Rest."

"Good, so you remember why you are here then?"

"The owl brought me. Guardian Grove was burnin'..." Her eyes were finally adjusting, and she could get a good look at the woman. Her hair hung over her tanned shoulders and was so covered in beads and feathers that it almost hid its rusty hue. She wore so many braided, colorful necklaces, they were all tangling together and looked like one big knot. Plain-brown cloth draped over her pudgy chest and legs, held on with a rope belt, and she was barefoot.

"Yes, dear, but I don't think we need to worry about that now. Do you know what happened to the Gypsy Witch?"

"No, she left o'er a week ago to take Cedric to Spring Meadows."

"Hmm... Then our worst fears are realized. We've never had to adjust to a new Guardian, but it must be done. Are you hungry, dear?"

"Yes'um... horribly so."

"Well, there's breakfast on the fire, and everyone has a load of questions for you. Our bark can be worse than our bite, and many of us are old and set in our ways... You came as quite a shock to us." She pointed a beefy finger under the bed at Coo'ara's feet. "There's clothes under there. As a Guardian, it's time you looked like one. Come on out when you're ready."

"Wait, who are..." The woman had already left, letting the woven mat fall back over the opening with a dull thuawp. "...you?" Coo'ara heard voices outside but could only make out bits of words that didn't make much sense to her. Reaching under the low bed, she pulled out a small bundle of clothes. They had obviously been freshly washed and smelled like the apula blossoms the Witch used to bring to her, and she wondered how long she had been asleep if they'd had time to wash clothes for her.

She took off her ragged dress and carefully folded it and put it on the bed. It was one of the only things she had that her mother had made for her, and even if it was torn and dirty, she wasn't ready to wad it up just yet. Holding up the new clothes, she couldn't believe that they were for her, or that anyone would let her wear them. It was very modest as the top, a simple straight neckline and long sleeves, nearly white with red embroidery of leaves chasing each other from one sleeve across to the other on a hand-stitched wind. The bottom had three layers, from white to rich orange to crimson red, each independent from the last. She looked around, expecting the woman to come back and tell her she had given her the wrong dress, but slid it on over her head excitedly when she didn't. It was so incredibly soft, like sleeping in the owl's downy nest, that she took a moment just to run her hands up and down the sleeves.

"I hope I can wear this every day." She took a deep breath in and held it, pushing past the mat and into the light.

Chapter Forty-Six

Not a single person in all of Spring Meadows wasn't trying to cram their way into the overly decorated cathedral on that fate-filled day, overflowing onto the cobblestone streets in droves. Every shop had closed early as anyone in their right mind had gotten all their shopping done the day before. Pale-pink flowers and clovers covered anything they could, from the lamp posts in the street to the edges of the aisle on pedestals, even draped from the ceiling in long flowing strands. A gentle harp played from somewhere in the upper balcony, barely being heard over the subdued roar of excited chatter.

Korva stood at the altar, sweat pouring so heavily from his forehead, he was sure everyone could see it. He suddenly became extremely thankful that Petal's handmaidens had chosen a black velvet cloak for him to wear; anything else and his nervousness would have stained it horribly. It seemed like a thousand women wearing fancy, lacey hats must all be muttering about him, about how awful he had been, how he didn't deserve to be standing there marrying their queen.

Strings and drums starting up from above quieted the crowd, and a choir of children began the hauntingly beautiful tones. Rain Dancer walked through the open doors, all of the mane braided in its stunning rainbow streaks, horn especially polished and glittering, juting through the base of it's bangs. With Petal side-saddle in her off-shoulder, white, rose-blossom dress. A carved wooden crown sat softly on her blonde hair, with sections just above her ears braided back in twisting, knotted patterns. The white veil hung over her face and over the back of Rain Dancer, delicate images of roses and clovers lining the sides. Every eye was on her, a most perfect being atop a winged horse clip-clopping down the stone aisle. Korva had never in his life seen anyone so beautiful, so beyond beauty and into perfection, she must have descended from the Mother herself.

As they came upon the altar, three men in white robes offered to help her down, but Petal ignored them and dismounted on her own. Korva held out his hand, and she took it to guide herself up the two small steps. He realized too late that he had the biggest, dumb grin on his face, and Petal giggled softly at him.

"Are you ready?" she whispered.

"I've been ready for ages."

"Ahem." The old man behind the altar cleared his throat before consulting the oversized book that lay open before him. "Ladies and Gentlemen... we are gathered here on this beautiful day, to witness the joining of souls between our dear queen, Colla Tep'um, and her chosen love... bound together as one being forevermore in our most holy and sacred of rites. Let us all remember this day, let us tell our children of this day, let us write this down in our book of history as the day our queen chose a king to rule beside her, at long last. Do you, Queen Petal Dancer, grant this man your hand and your bed, until the day the Mother takes back your soul?"

"I give him my hand, as a promise to stand with him in all things," She grabbed his hand and blushed, "to always and forevermore take him to be my king."

"And do you, Korva, grant our queen your hand and your bed, until the day the Mother takes back your soul?"

"I give her my hand, my life, and my soul, to stand beside her forevermore, to make her my queen in all things."

"Then I do declare you are now joined. From this day forth, may you live happily in each other's arms, and let no man nor beast come between you. In the name of the Mother, go in peace." He closed the book with a dusty thump, and Korva delicately lifted the thin vale from Petal's face, casting it over her head. He stared into her soft-gray eyes as his hand grazed her cheek, on the edge of joyful tears.

"They forgive you," Petal whispered and kissed Korva. The room exploded in cheers and clapping as hats and flowers were thrown into the air, hanging there for a moment before falling to the floor.

***

"Seers? What are seers?" Coo'ara asked the circle of men as they finished their scrambled eggs on wooden plates. Every time one of them spoke, their feathers shifted and flowed, like their hair was made only of them.

"Not so much Seers as one Seer and her Keepers, child. It is said they tend to the new growth of the Mother's roots, beyond the edges of our world in the Borderlands. Most believed they were a myth, an invention of imagination." The oldest man with the most feathers swirled his hand through the air as he spoke.

"A myth until one showed up here about a day or so ago." The portly woman stacked the empty plates. "Poor thing looked on the rim of death, but they insisted they had to get to the Mother. Let me at least feed them before they went on." She took a metal kettle off the coals and poured a black liquid into wooden cups before passing them out. It smelled earthy and deep, and even though she was thirsty, Coo'ara couldn't imagine being able to drink it. "If what she said was true, the war is far from over."

"What did she say?"

"She left us a prophecy, the darkness that we think has passed has not... Our whole world is about to change. I've been trying to send a raven to the Gypsy Witch, but if she was beyond the Hunter's Camp in the forest, that would explain why it returned undelivered."

"If the Witch is dead, we need to prepare for our new Guardian to take her place. We need to present her to the people." Men shook their heads in disagreement.

"Without her body, we cannot confirm her death."

"But Wind Runner has chosen another. Is that not confirmation enough for you, old man? Our Witch is gone. We must make do with the child."

"You don't have to talk about me like I'm not here. I know I'm not your first choice for a

Guardian, but please understand I didn't do this. I didn't mean for this to happen."

"Oh child, we know you didn't." The woman gave Coo'ara a kind smile before pointing a chunky finger at each of the men in turn. "You men need to remember your place. She may be a child, but she holds more power than you could ever hope to see." They knew they were being scolded and fiddled with their fingers or twirled their feathers. "Now, don't you all have things you need to do besides doubting her worth?" The group dispersed, only the old man remaining to help the woman bed down the fire.

Coo'ara wasn't exactly sure what she should be doing, but she felt like she should be helping. As soon as she stood and tried to grab the plates however, the woman shooed her away.

"You don't need to be doing all that, child. Why don't you go to our history keepers and read up on your people? We are only one tribe of these lands, and each will expect you to know their own ways and customs when you are presented. They are just over there, with the blue in their doorway."

Chapter Forty-Seven

Tom could finally see the outline of huts and tents through the mist over the next hill. several weeks after they had left the Mother Tree, the cart dragging behind an exhausted, brown horse. Autumn Fall had always been one of his favorite places to visit, normally vibrant with its golds and reds painted over every tree in their perfect rows, but today, the sky was filled with tall, gray clouds. A light drizzle had soaked him to the bone, and they took the nauseating hills one step at a time. It was like the whole land knew why he was there and wept for its lost Guardian as thunder rumbled off in the distance.

"Mother, I hope we get there before this storm truly hits." The horse knickered in agreement, trying its best to keep up the pace as they started up the last hill. "C'mon, old boy. I think this is the last one."

Their arrival did not go unnoticed. News spread quicker than wildfire, and crowd had formed at the top of the hill. They whispered among themselves but grew quiet when Tom and the cart reached the top. The clear block of magic ice was still solid even after the long trip, and inside, the body of the Gypsy Witch laid peacefully in its everlasting sleep. Some cried, holding bits of fabric to their faces to dry their eyes, while others moaned dramatically, asking the Mother for mercy and comfort. Tom slowly unhitched the horse and let it walk off unburdened for the first time in weeks.

"There is no amount of thanks I can offer you for this journey you have made. Please tell us your name so it can be remembered." The oldest man with feathers cascading down his back bowed in respect to Tom.

"There is no need for all that. I remember when my king was killed, the need from the people to have a proper burial... well, it only felt right to return her here."

"We can begin to heal now. Please, traveler, let us feed you before you go on your way."

"If I could, I would, but I'm afraid I have to be going sooner rather than later. The new Winter King should be taking his throne, and I have an awful feeling about the whole thing."

"At least let us wrap something for you, it would be most unkind of us to see you go without something as thanks. That, and Tibera will murder me herself if I see you off without food." Tom chuckled at the old man and allowed himself to be led into the little village. He towered over everyone and even most of the tents and huts, and he was soon surrounded with people who had obviously never seen a giant from the north before.

"Tibera! Tibera, wrap a meal for this man. He has brought our Witch home to rest." The old man called out to a stout, pudgy woman who stirred something green in a large, black pot over a fire. She looked over, then up at Tom, taken aback for a moment at his sheer size.

"Well now, that is wonderful news! What is your name, giant?"

"Just call me Tom, miss. Your Guardian died protecting the Mother from the darkness. She was braver than any man I have known."

"She was always a brave protector, an example to be followed. Quite an odd name that is, Tom… It will sound funny when we tell of your story by the fire."

"Call me whatever you like. I've never been one for recognition. Say she walked here for all that it matters."

"Oh no, whether you like it or not, giant, our children will hear of your selflessness. Can you not stay for a meal? Sapling soup is my specialty."

"I'm afraid I can't. I have to get back to the Winterlands, see how our new king is faring."

"You are going to see the King of Winter? You have quite the walk ahead of you then. Give me a moment to make a sack for you. I'm afraid it won't be much given your size."

"No need to worry, miss. I'm a fairly good trapper once I'm in my natural environment."

"Would you mind terribly bringing something with you? The ravens have been rather unpredictable lately, and I can't trust them to go all the way into the mountains."

"Of course, may I ask what it is?" She stopped her stirring and dried her hands on her dress.

"What do you know of Seers?"

"Well, I know the legends. Can't say I've ever met one."

"Then you know of their ability to foretell the future?"

"I've heard they have warned many before disaster befell them, yes."

"Well, one came here. She and her keepers, and they passed on their prophesy so that we may prepare. It makes little sense to us, and our new Guardian... she is very young. Perhaps someone else can make sense of it?"

"I can't say if Cedric will understand it either, but his advisors will want to see it." Tibera nodded.

"That will have to do. Just send word if anything is learned."

"Indeed. I will make sure of it."

Chapter Forty-Eight

Bitter cold, biting wind beat against the solid stone of the Winterland stronghold, as high in the mountains as was possible to live. It was carved directly from the stone of the mountain with no windows, and a solid steel door kept the Winterland chill at bay. Very few dared to venture this high into the mountains and even fewer dared to attack the impregnable fortress. To date, only one had ever been successful.

When Cedric arrived at the doors, they opened inward before he could even dismount to knock, as if they had been awaiting his arrival. Several men had been rushing back and forth through the hall, all of which stopped in their tracks as the doors creaked open. They saw a vision of old, the Winter King in full armor riding the mighty Snow Bringer into the hall, as if no time had passed since his death, and he was simply returning from a hunting trip. They knew in their hearts that Frost Slayer was long gone but couldn't deny their eyes, thus dropping to their knees.

"My Lord, you have returned." A thin, brown-haired man knelt and presented his hands.

"I... I think you have the wrong man." Cedric almost chuckled, but he could see where the confusion would come from. His white beard and hair had grown long, covering part of the blank chest plate and nearly all of his back, and his blue eyes were icy and cold as he looked down on the advisers.

The thin man rose wearily, rubbing his face as he tried to focus. The doors swinging closed and the dim fire from torches on the walls became the only light again.

"Forgive me, you are a spitting image of our Frost Slayer. I fear we have gone many years without him, and some here could feel we had a Guardian again... We assumed he had been remade." Cedric dismounted, and the man could now see the small differences. Cedric was a bit shorter than their king had been, and the scars that crisscrossed his face were a dead giveaway.

"I am Cedric, son of Frost and Ember."

"Son!" The man suddenly became excited, as did many others as whispers hummed all around them. "A blood heir of Winter, oh, this is tremendous news! Tell me how you know of your claim?"

"The Witch of Autumn Fall, she told me she was there when I was born."

"The Witch, indeed. Then it must be true, our prayers have been answered!" He rose his arms into the air, and his voice echoed through the stone cavern of a hall. "We have a Guardian and a king! Hail the Mother, she hears our cry from the highest mount!" There was screaming, hollers of celebration, and cries of relief as people came from the tunnels and behind hidden doors. Women lifted their children, and men threw their fur hats into the air. There were hundreds of people living in the mountain, and they all wanted to get a first glance at the new king.

"Please forgive us, My Lord. The Winterlands have suffered greatly in the absence of a king. Many battles have been fought over small bits of land, and refugees flocked to our stronghold to save their families from slaughter. Come, let me take you to the throne room. Let them praise your coming in a less crowded space."

Cedric wanted to protest; he hadn't been able to get much sleep in the past weeks as they had walked day and night to get here. All he wanted was to lie down, but more than one set of hands had grabbed his arms and directed him through heavy, stone doors. Snow Bringer knickered but wandered off down a tunnel on his own accord.

The throne itself seemed to have formed out of the ground in jutting shards, thick plates of ice fanning out behind in an impressive display of power. The arms were miniature sculptures of Snow Bringer, the heads grazing near their six hooves. Cedric circled it slowly, running his gloved hand over the sharp points of the back. Only one other king had ever sat here, his father proud and strong, and now it was his turn. He removed the ice sword from his side, and he could see one of the horses had a space to hold it as the neck curled around. As he sat, the people cheered, and he could feel their pride in him rising like a fire in his gut. He raised a fist into the air.

"Long live the king! Guardian! Lord! Long live he!"

He pulled off his gloves and touched the snowflake on his Kra, dissolving his icy armor. The thin man walked up to him holding a white pillow with a tall ice crown sitting lightly on it.

"Today, we are thankful for this moment, thankful for this opportunity to rebuild our great realm, to bond it together under a flag of new hope." He handed the cushion to a boy and lifted the crown from it. "This has seen no other head, kept safe in our vaults, knowing that one day it would see our rightful king once more." He placed it on Cedric's head, crowning him as the King of the Winterlands for all the stronghold to see. The spikes rose high, shards of ice molded together and catching the firelight from the torches. Cedric sighed deeply, the celebrations around him flowing together in a constant roar. The people blurred together as they came up to him, swearing their loyalty to him.

His ears rang, and the activity of the room seemed to slow, then stopped entirely. Cedric waved a hand in front of the man kneeling at his feet, but it was like he was frozen. The fire in his gut burned like he had swallowed a hot coal, and the ringing grew to a crippling level. He could feel hot blood dripping from his ears as he screamed in pain.

"I told you I couldn't be destroyed, Cedric," the slithery voice whispered from inside his head. *"You were born in me, and you are part of me. I am darkness, and you are but a simple man. Submit to me, and I will spare your mind."*

Sound and movement returned to the hall, and the man in front of Cedric finished his speech of loyalty and moved back into the crowd. No one seemed to notice the moment that Cedric had experienced, and it became harder to believe by the second that it had even happened. The pain in his gut disappeared as quickly as it came, and after feeling his ears for the blood he knew he had felt dripping down his cheek and finding nothing, he tried to chalk it up to exhaustion.

"My mind must be playing tricks on me."

"What did you say, My King?"

"Nothing. Everything is fine. I believe I just need some sleep."

"Yes, you have traveled far to grace us with your presence. I will call for your room to be made." The thin man turned to talk to a group of women, who rushed off with small nods.

"Thank you, you have given us hope for the coming days."

"I pray I will be able to deliver on your hope."

Epilogue

The embers, now practically cold to the touch, cumbled against each other on the cooling brick, collapsing into nothing but grey dust. The sun was just beginning to peek through the dainty lace curtains over the window, casting beams of light onto dinner plates stacked high in the sink in the kitchen. The little boy slept comfortably, wrapped in a freshly finished quilt in his great-grandmother's arms, his soft snores one of the only sounds in the near silent room. She smiled as she looked around at her family, the wrinkles of her face softening as her heart swelled. Every single one of them, from the mothers in aprons to the old men in suits with pipes in their pockets, had fallen asleep leaning on each other draped throughout her dining room.

"I guess I'll have to continue this story at another time." She whispered, gently placing the boy and the quilt next to his father who had fallen asleep at her feet. She traced the outline of the Mother Tree, admiring her own work on the quilt before shuffling to the window. Pulling back the curtain with a shaking hand, she watched as snowflakes floated down through the rays of light as they peaked through the frosted evergreens outside. "Soon winter will be over," she said to herself, "maybe fall will come again." Her gray eyes sparkled with happiness.

Made in the USA
Columbia, SC
27 January 2023